PRISONERS

PRISONERS

a novel by
Dorothy Bryant

Ata Books
Berkeley, California

Ata Books
1928 Stuart Street
Berkeley, California 94703

Cover design: Robert K. Bryant

*For my good friend
and discerning critic
Betty Bacon*

THE CORRESPONDENCE BETWEEN
SALLY MORGAN AND GARY WILSON
PRESERVED FOR PRESENTATION TO HER
ON THE DAY HIS FREEDOM IS WON

December 27

Miss Sarah Morgan
10 Crown Court
Berkeley, California

Dear Miss Morgan:

To convey appreciation of your Christmas Card comprises the purpose of this letter. My assumption being you acquired my name and address from the Free Weekly. i hope to develop correspondence with respect to exchange of mutual aspirations and hope's. Eventually perhaps even to discover shared value's in common.

Very sincerely your's,

Gary Wilson

Jan 2

Dear Gary Wilson,

Yes, I'd be glad to write to you, but I want to make sure I don't do so under false pretences. Let me explain. I sent Christmas cards to all fifteen of the prisoners listed in the Free Weekly as wanting to correspond with people outside. I heard from five (besides you). Two asked for large sums of money, one asked me to establish a bank account under my name where his friend could deposit money (loot? get-away money?) and the other two were interested only in letters from girls under twenty-five. I had to disappoint all five of them, and I don't want to mislead anyone else.

The sad truth is I am fifty years old, a middle-aged, middle-class Berkeley housewife with two grown children, a dog, three cats, six fish, two turtles and, probably, numerous mice. Lately I have done some reading about prison conditions, and I'm not quite over the shock. I am ashamed when I think of how I have let myself remain ignorant of the obvious wrong of imprisonment for so long. And as I write these words, I begin to ask myself, how can I presume to write anything at all to you? What have I to say? I don't think I have ever felt quite so helpless and useless before.

Sincerely,

Sally Morgan

1

Wednesday
January 5

Dear Sally Morgan,

You're letter was extremly amusing. Little is discovered to be productive of laughter on these premises. So, contrary to you're supositions already you have been of assistence.

The men who wrote to you are typical. When time stretches out far in the future with inconsequentil hope and ultimate alienation into solitary despare. So consequently they enhance fantasies of escape or sex or material benifets of the consumption standard of living. Or revenge, which consumated my fantasies during my seven or eight months of initial incarceration in this facility.

But then i suddently realized the danger of eminent decay of my faculties. To turn my sentence into a death sentence of my brain. (Which is what some people want) So consequently i disavowed futile fantasy. i commenced a self-imposed program of reading, then writing. And the stimulation of discorse with other few prisoners with similarity of thought (dangerous in terms of evidential rehabilitation and eventual release).

Also dangerous might be your comment on the injustice of imprisonment. It could be deamed evident that you're letters do not militate towards a constructive force in my rehabilitation. Rehabilitation is a frequently operative expression in this facility. Meaning something very differnt to me than to the people who say they are rehabilitating me. But i have already said too much.

My books, my writing, my thinking has taken my supine brain and uplifted it out of the decay of despair. But am i merly in another cell? sheltered in isolation from the desolation surrounding me. A self-imposed solitary confinement (said condition referred to as Adjustment Center here).

So you see why i need someone from outside to write to me. i don't care how old you are or how you live. i remain fervently convinced that two people can transend age or other considerations. The mere fact that you have written to me gives ample evidence of you're elevation beyond predjudicial attitudes of mundane personalities.

Write to me about anything. About your pets. We are not allowed to keep living creaturs as companions in our cells. Not even plants. But i have outwitted the authorities. In the ceiling corner above my bunk lives a large spider. i call her Esmerelda. She sits

2

waiting and watching. i am endeavering to assimilate her genius, to learn how to wait and watch too.

Unfortunately other living things share my cell. Occcasionally fumigation takes place, and these creaturs hide. Presumably suffering indisposition from a bad cough and then return. i wrote a long poem once to a bedbug, after i found one in the library that a famous poet wrote about a flea.

Best wishes,

Gary W.

P.S. i extend apologies for my spelling. The library is closed today baring me from consultation with the dictionary. However, i desired no delay in sending this, hoping for early reply.

Sunday 1/9

Dear Gary,

My biggest pet is Yossarian, who is a German Shepherd, rather small for a male, brown and black, with white fur all down his hind-quarters, so that he looks a bit like an old fashioned 18th century gentleman in pantaloons (sometimes he acts that way too). Yossarian started out to be John's (my son) dog. He got him as a puppy, six years ago. John was reading *Catch-22* at the time and named him after the hero. My husband Bob says that Yossarian quite rightfully decided not to forgive John for giving him that name, considering what Yossarian went through in that book, and that's why he has nothing to do with John. Bob says Yossarian was marked from birth by that name. He is very solemn, as if remembering a deep sorrow. His moods run from glum to sad, to resigned, to — at his very manic height I would say Yossarian is dignified. When he lost interest in John, he began to show suspicion toward all young people. He will have nothing to do with children. If one approaches him, he quietly gets up and walks to the other side of the room. If the child persists, Yossarian will scare him away with a short but businesslike bark. (Unfortunately this problem doesn't arise often anymore—we've reached the age where we hardly ever have children around). He is rather hostile toward men though he endures Bob. He is indifferent to other dogs (except the female Siberian Huskie down the street—he madly loves her, but since she is at least triple his size, any attempt to

3

demonstrate his affection makes him look ridiculous and hence even more solemn) which is probably good because there are so many dogs in Berkeley it is impossible to walk a block without encountering a dozen.

Yossarian follows me wherever I go. He's lying across my feet now. He takes me for walks; I love to walk, especially at night or very early in the morning when I can't sleep, and if one walks at such times, it's best to be accompanied by a large dog. He sits in the corner of whatever room I am working in, seeming always to be lost in his own sad thoughts, but really very alert and watchful. I would get a great ego boost from his devotion if it were not that I suspect he sees himself as much older and wiser than I, and what I take for blind animal devotion is really the patient vigil of a baby sitter.

The cats are, of course, full of catlike egotism and independence, except for Molly, the neurotic little gray one who was weaned too soon and therefore tries to nurse on anyone who sits beside her. Benjamin is striped red and white, tigerish and proud. He is always jumping up on the dining room table, then standing there in a lean, languid pose, waiting for us to admire him before someone sweeps him off onto the floor. Nicholas is the oldest of the three and the only one intentionally gotten. (The others just walked in on us, as most of our cats do. We always have at least three, once eight or nine, I'm not sure; that time I lost count.) Nicholas is about five years old, all black and very large. Nicholas is paranoid. He will not let anyone touch him. If anyone even thinks of petting Nicholas, he senses the threat and disappears. The other cats, even silly little Molly, stay far away from him. Deep behind Nicholas's paranoia, however, is some drive toward love. When I come home, he hears my car, and before I get the door open, he is sitting out on the curb. He walks me into the house (I don't touch him, of course, or he would run away) and then disappears.

I'm allergic to cats, and during the summer months especially (with pollen added to the problem) I get red nosed and miserable. But I can't bear to turn them out and have decided that the physical discomfort is worth the spiritual nourishment I get from them.

The fish are no more. I came home to an overturned bowl, a puddle of water on the floor, and no fish. All three cats looked fiercely innocent, even Molly.

The turtles, Freud and Jung, live in the back yard, which climbs up and down the side of a hill. Sometimes they get tired, I guess, of all

4

those ups and downs, and have to be rounded up, brought home from one of the more level neighbors' yards. They are very useful for keeping down the bugs, but our neighbors haven't been tempted to keep them when they stray because their own dogs simply go insane at the sight of one. Jung is actually rather fierce, and I've been told he clamped onto the leg of one dog who was bothering him and rode for half a block before letting go. But both turtles usually withdraw into their shells and I've never seen them do anything but "play rock" whenever anyone disturbs them.

Of course, tenant on the cats and Yossarian are thousands of fleas, but I haven't got round to naming them yet, and the way they bite all of us hasn't inspired me to anything like Donne's cleverness.

Sally

P.S. This seems such a stupid letter. Are you sure this is what you want? Is your mail really censored?

Tuesday, January 11

Dear Sally,

Yossarian is remeniscent of a grandiose german shepherd going back to my childhood, which i rode at the tender age of three years old. Gripping the hairs of his back, he sauntered down Army Street where i lived, in the Mission District of San Francisco. This area comprises a section of San Francisco you doubtless never heard of. It possessing neither the big hotels of Nob Hill or the bridges or any other postcard portrait of The City. Not even the fog. Of which the people of the Mission take pride in, the presence of larger quantities of sunshine. Little else exists for them to take pride in. (When such comes into existence, they move out of the Mission). Oh, yes, they take pride in being mostly white, although they are not very white, being mostly chicano now.

i must discomfortedly confess to sharing such pride and looking down on the black people who inhabited the other side of Market Street or over Potrero Hill at Hunter's Point. When i began to read i perceived the dialectic of the need of a spurious sense of superiority. A need of the economically deprived and despised. With this perception arrived total loss of hate for those i once deemed my inferiors. Now i only hate injustice and oppression. i hate men who

5

imprison other men and grind them down, humiliate and perform unspeakable atrocities in the name of sacred rehabilitation.

In answer to you'r question about my mail. No, of course my mail is not censored. This is an enlightened institution. Notice it is not even called a prison. It is a Farm. Or facility. A wholesome title for a wholesome institution. My mail is privileged with privacy. But for some infathomable reason i am forbidden to seal the envelope of this letter. This service being performed by the authorities for this Facility. No restrictions are placed on quantity sent or received. Incoming mail is not censored. No. But on many occcassians mysteriously is lost. For example, my copy of the Free Weekly, where i made contact with you, often gets lost, especially just after an announcement that the forthcoming issue will contain articles on prison conditions.

Nevertheless, please remain cognizant that i am very fortunate, having, for instance, a cell all to myself, six by eight feet, containing a bunk and a table and a lavatory facility in the corner. i sit on my bunk and write and revise. Then i borrow a typewriter from the man two cells down. Then i remove my books off the table and i place the typewriter on the table. Positioned on my bunk while typing, my knees bump against the table. When i exercise, i place table and books on the bunk, whereupon i perform push-ups, frequently grazing my head on the lavatory bowl.

i tolerate such frustrations with equanimaty. Worse is the noise which incessantly creates a barrage on the very soul. Last summer i awakened in the night, thinking i would be driven insane by the excruciating and obscene noises of this institution. To keep my sanity, i took a pencil and made a list of the noises. Later i showed it to a writer (inmate) who called it a poem. i said, "it is not a poem, it is a list of things that are driving me crazy." And he said, "That is a good definition of a poem."

My dear Sally, i have placed you in number one position on the short list of things which will keep me sane. Please write again soon.

Gary

P.S. This time i was able to consult a dictionary in the library, and i hope my spelling is better. i am endeavoring diligently to improve my writing and increase my vocabulary. i would appreciate any corrections and suggestions you could make regarding my spelling, grammar, etc.

6

Dear Gary,

So you grew up in San Francisco. Somehow I thought, because you're in Southern California now, that you had not lived in the Bay Area. Bob was born in the Mission District too, and has told me many stories and shown me places where he lived and went to school, so that I feel I know the area well although I have always lived in Berkeley (sometimes I think I must be the only native Berkeleyan living here!).

When Bob was a boy, the Mission was mostly populated by Irish and Italians. Latin Americans were not there in large numbers until World War II. Perhaps you and Bob attended the same schools. He went to Starr King. He would have gone on to Mission High, but his family was very poor, and so he left school and worked until the war. He finished high school in the service and then went to UC on the GI Bill. (That was where we met.) Bob says that when he meets old Missionites, they talk about the good old days in the Mission District (what good old days? says Bob) and then they complain about how the Mission has "gone down," whatever that means. (All these people, you understand, now live in tracts on the penninsula) Bob says the Germans and Swedes who were moving out when his family came said the same thing.

But occasionally we visit a sculptor who lives just above Mission High School and, getting there, we pass a coffee house, a storefront Chicano political club, and several bookstores. Once we attended a mime show at the old community center where Bob used to stand in line for free milk during the Depression. I find the mixture exciting, but for Bob the area holds too many memories.

I'm not qualified to advise you on your writing, but I'll try to help. I once did some tutoring in a class of young people, and it seemed to me that many of their problems came from lack of confidence, which made them search for very long words and elaborate sentences which they thought were superior to their normal way of speaking. I found that when I could get a person to forget all that and to write in his own normal way, with his own words, direct and simple, why, most of the grammar problems just disappeared. Who was the famous writer who said, never use a long word when a short word will do?

Sorry this must be cut short. I promised to cover the city council meeting for the Free Weekly, as their regular reporter is sick. That's the only kind of writing I do now, and I deeply admire anyone who can turn pain and frustration into poetry. I hope some day you'll let me read some of your poems.

In haste,

Sally

Dear Sally,

Your husband left the Mission to go to war, and my parents came. They were called Okies. They were very poor like people in "The Grapes of Wrath." (The first book i read here) They worked at Hunter's Point shipyard's. They had one kid, my brother. He went to Alaska. i have not seen him for ten years. After the war was over hard times came again. My mother got pregnant. My father left. i never saw him. She heard he died two year's ago.

She moved into the Army Street housing project. We were on welfare. When i started school mother went to work, housework. Now she is a live-in maid for some rich people in Pacific Heights or i think maybe Seacliff.

i was the fastest reader in my fourth grade class. But i slowed down. i spent more time in the principal's office than the class. i was always getting into fights, mostly with an Italian kid who called me Okie, or a black kid i called nigger. Not with chicano's. They would stand and watch us beat each other while they took over the neighborhood. Some teachers liked me anyway. Miss McLeod used to say be a good boy. Once she took me and two girls for a ride to Berkeley to show us the campus. She said if we studied hard and were good that's where we would end up.

In junior high i started to hate the teachers and they started to hate me. i think they started first. i guess they all wanted to teach on the other side of town. Where there were no Okie's and no Chicano's. One or two were okay. But i was too far gone, i guess.

So i never made it to Mission High either. Just like your husband. No, not just like him. i got thrown out of school for hitting a teacher. Suspended for two weeks. i just never went back. No one ever came looking for me. i guess they were glad to get rid of me.

After that i just hung around the streets. Now rich or middle-class (all the same when you're poor) kids drop out and say school is like a prison. i felt like that but i did not know it. i could not say the things i really knew inside. And no one else said them. All they said was i was no good if i did not keep quiet and stay in school and do what they told me. i really tried. i couldn't. i just blew up. i did not know why. So i believed them. i was no good.

i was always ashamed that i didn't finish school. i didn't want you to know. Reading about your husband i got the courage to tell you. Maybe some day i will go back to school like he did. But i will never go back to The Mission even if your sculptor friend likes it. It is a battleground where i bled and died. Or thought i died.

Now i know about your dog and your husband. i still do not know much about you.

Waiting for your next letter,

Gary

P.S. Is this what you mean? i tried to use simple words, the way i talk (without the profanity). It looks pretty dumb to me. But now you know i'm an uneducated bum, so i might as well not try to use long words to hide it.

Tuesday 1/25

Dear Gary,

I don't think there's anything very interesting to tell about me. I was born in Berkeley half a century ago (I had to write it that way; it boggles my mind to think it, and it almost seems I could tame the thought by writing it out). Berkeley was a very quiet little town then. My father taught at the university, and my mother used to take me for walks, pushing me in a perambulator (as they were called in those days) along the paths through the campus. We would end up at my father's office or outside his classroom, give him a wave or a kiss, and then go on home, to a brown-shingled, vine-covered house on a lot covered with trees (since torn down and replaced by an apartment house) just south of campus. For a long time I thought of the campus as an extension of our backyard.

I graduated from Berkeley High and went to the university. I expect that if the war hadn't come, I would have gone on pretty much as my father planned, majoring in English like him and going on to graduate school.

9

When the war started, I left school and went to work in the shipyards in Richmond. (While your parents worked at Hunter's Point, I was doing the same kind of work just across the Bay.) Of course it took quite a lot of determination on my part to do this, and my father never recovered from my rebellion. In a way I never recovered either. The Richmond shipyards were my first taste of real life. I met a different kind of people there, poor people, hard-working people from all over the country. My father hoped that seeing and doing such hard work would make me value the academic life more, but this last hope of his was futile. I met an old wobbly who used to talk to me during lunch. He didn't quite convert me to socialism, but, between him and the other people I saw every day, I began to realize that something was very wrong with the arrangement of our lives, and that people had proposed alternatives to this arrangement.

When the war ended I went back to UC, but by this time I knew that I was not a scholar. People excited me just as much as books did. I met Bob, who was struggling along on his GI bill money and seeing the university as a heaven he had never hoped to reach. I did the only sensible thing: I married Bob and went to work to put him through school. He now teaches in a junior high school here in Berkeley.

We have two children—well, not children anymore, of course. My daughter Nancy is twenty-six and my son John must be about the same age as you, 24. My son, by the way, got fed up with school by the tenth grade, so I'm not at all shocked by your leaving school. I'm only surprised so many young people put up with the dullness of school as I did. I'm more ashamed of that kind of docility than I would be of rebellion against the inane things done in the name of education.

So there you have it. I'm a housewife, doing the usual PTA things, putting in some time to help along some good causes, but not accomplishing anything to speak of.

Sally

P.S. Yes, I think your last letter is very well written, not dumb at all, more natural. Now you could get rid of some extra apostrophes. Oh, and I (when you mean yourself) should be capitalized. I assume you want me to tell you these things because writing is so important to you, though I'm the last one who should correct you. Dennis (a friend of mine who teaches writing) says I write like a woman running downhill carrying buckets of water, propelled forward and spilling all over. That's because I always seem to be behind schedule, rushing to catch up, and never having a minute to proofread let alone recast a sentence!

Friday
January 28

Dear Sally,

Yes, please go on helping correct my writing. i try to use a dictionary when i rewrite my letters (i could never send you the first draft) but i cant always get to the library.

i know i should be I. i read e.e. cummings last year and i stopped capitalizing everything. Then i started to use capitals again but not to mean myself. i guess i don't feel like a capital I. Maybe some day i will.

i could never understand the apostrophe so i put one in everywhere just in case. Then a funny coincidence—when your letter came, i was reading G.B. Shaw. Shaw did not use the apostrophe at all. He thought it was a stupid mark. I agree with him, and i am not going to waste my time learning to use it "correctly." Like using the right spoon in the house of the rich people my mother works for. i am a prisoner, but in this way i can be free. Free of convention. (Tell me if i misused that word—up until i saw it in Shaw i thought it meant a big meeting.)

i guess i wasted a lot of time looking up long words in the dictionary and using them to try and make my writing look educated. But now i will follow your advice and stick to my own words.

The funny thing is, it is just as hard to write a letter when i dont use big words. i still have to go over and over a sentence to make sure it says what i mean.

You do not really want to read my poems. Youre too busy to waste your time on that garbage.

i like your story of how you left the university and went to work in the shipyards. That makes you a drop-out just like me. (Just kidding) Your mother and father must have been very upset when you quit again, after you met your husband. i bet they hoped that even if you did not finish college you would marry a college professor, like your father. But you married a lower class man, put him through school, so he could rise. Sally, i can read between the lines of your letter and see you are not the routine "housewife, doing the usual PTA things." No, you are much more. i think you must be a very beautiful person.

11

It is time for me to tell you why i am here. You have not asked. But you must wonder. Maybe you think you could be writing to a murderer or a rapist. But you are too sensitive to ask. i think you have a right to know.

i am here for nothing.

i know what you are thinking. The old joke about how all men in prison are innocent. But when i explain, i think you will agree. i will explain it all.

After i left school, i was a pretty wild kid. All i did was drive up and down the Dolores Street hill in whatever car i could strip down and rev up. i was king of the world with a can of beer in one hand and the steering wheel in the other. i took money my mother earned scrubbing floors, to buy gas or parts for my ego-on-wheels. She gave me the money because she was afraid i would get in worse trouble without it. i am not proud of that, but i want you to know it. It is the worst thing i did, and if i am being punished for something, i like to believe it is for all the times i made my mother cry. My prison sentence makes more sense that way.

One day i was cruising down Mission Street. I heard someone yell my name. i stopped. It was two friends of mine. They jumped into the car. "Go, man!" i didn't notice theyd been running. i drove down Mission, and they said drive on to this bar in Daly City. We were almost there when they told me. They had just robbed a liquor store on Eighteenth Street.

Then i heard the siren. They threw their guns out of the car, but it was too late. i tried to tell the police i had nothing to do with it, but no one believed me. My so-called friends said they told me before they got into the car. Maybe they thought they did. The public defender said i should plead guilty to driving the getaway car and he could get me probation, but if i pled innocent i would be found guilty of armed robbery and be put away with the other guys. i pled guilty and got probation.

But my probation officer hated me. He hounded me until he got enough on me to revoke probation and put me away. The excuse he used was a fight i got into in a bar.

That is what i mean when i say i am here for nothing. i have been here for twenty months and two days. This institution is supposed to rehabilitate me. How can i be rehabilitated by injustice? How can i keep myself from feeling the rage they say proves i am not rehabilitated? Do i lie to prove i am rehabilitated? But if i say i am

12

innocent, that proves i am not rehabilitated. They are stealing my life, day by day, but i must they are right and thank them for what they are doing to me, before they will even think of letting me out.

Enough. i am soon eligible for my second parole application, and i should not be writing this (though of course, no one reads the letters i am not allowed to seal).

i am sending you, in a separate envelope, copies of all my documents, so that you will know i am telling you the truth about all this. i just wanted you to know. i try not to think about it. If i did i would go out of my mind. That is why i try to read, to write, to keep myself in good physical condition (i exercise, even in my cell, eat no flesh, and spend whatever money i can get on nuts and fruits—the food here would ruin the most healthy body). And that is why your letters mean so much to me.

Tell me more about yourself. Do you live near Telegraph Avenue? i hear that middle-class drop-outs line the street begging. If they had ever been poor they would do anything but beg.

You write sometimes for the Free Weekly? Then you must know the editor. Next time you go to the Free Weekly office, ask if he ever prints writing by prisoners.

As ever,

Gary

Thurs. 2/3

Dear Gary,

I've read all your documents and passed them on to a lawyer friend of mine. I'd like to reserve comment on all of that until I hear from him.

I've sent you a dictionary. We had several around the house, and it seemed silly that you should have to go to the library every time you wanted to check a word. It should get to you within a few days.

I suppose we're not far from Telegraph Avenue, since Berkeley is a small town and you can walk to any part of it (unless you're struggling uphill) within half an hour. We live on the other side of the campus, the north side, which puts us psychologically rather far from Telegraph. We live in a little dead-end street just off Spruce, halfway up the hill, a short loop called Crown Court. We live in the bow of the horseshoe loop, and from the street you can hardly see our house. It climbs up the side of the hill and is quite hidden by trees and shrubs.

To get to our house, you have to climb up a path, then a series of winding stone steps (absolute hell on a rainy day carrying bags of groceries). Finally you get to the front porch. Two steps up to the living room, across, three steps up to the kitchen, one step down to the dining room. There are two bedrooms upstairs (one for Bob and me; the other he uses as his study) and two bedrooms downstairs. My son is here now temporarily, staying in his room. My daughter is married, and far away, so her room is empty, but my mother uses it when she visits. There's one other room, beneath the lower bedrooms, almost at the street level, but because of the peculiar structure of the house, it can only be reached from inside. So, one climbs down and down to what we call the Dungeon. It's a pretty little room, and I often come down here (that's where I am now) to sew or read or write, or just to find a little peace and quiet.

The trouble with our house is that not only are all the rooms on separate levels, like cubes stuck into the side of the hill, but they are tipped every which way. (Set down a pencil or ball and it rolls to the other side of the room!) You see, we live on a very pretty slope, but in a slide area. We spend part of every year shoring things up, but the house still feels as if it is about to break apart and fall, room by room, into the street below. Of course, since it has stood for nearly fifty years there seems to be little real danger of that happening so long as we keep applying structural bandaids. The houses below, on either side of the horseshoe, all lean slightly downhill. There used to be a funny kind of togetherness every spring, when everyone was out propping things up and comparing the width of cracks and worrying together about heavy rains. But many of the original owners have moved out, renting the houses to groups of students, and we don't know as many of our neighbors as we used to. We've been here over twenty years, and perhaps we've come to see the house as symbolic. (What of depends on how good or how bad a day I'm having when I think about it.)

Your description of Telegraph Avenue is in part true. The scene started out to be picturesque, but became ugly with dope traffic. Now that seems to have slacked off and The Avenue is quieter but depressed. Beggars who are truly poor and homeless. Sleazy clothing sold in garish shops. Trashy street vendors. Grimy commercialism. (Maybe to tourists it's still picturesque.)

I hope you won't be shy about your poetry. I would love to read some of it, though I am ignorant, an enthusiastic if not very discriminating reader.

Best wishes,

Sally

P.S. The Free Weekly "office" is the basement of young (35) friends of mine. Yves and Mary Stewart edit it, along with doing most of the writing, proofreading, layout and selling. Volunteers come and go. Mary says they would be delighted to see work by prisoners.

P.P.S. You are a vegetarian? Of course, you're quite right. I wish I were thoughtful and disciplined enough to change my habits. But I'm concerned about your getting proper food. According to that list of rules you sent, I can't mail food to you, but I'm depositing a few dollars in your canteen account so you can buy more nuts. Wish I could do more.

Monday
February 7

Dear Sally.

Your dictionary will not reach me. Check your list of rules again. Number 16. Prisoners may receive books only directly from the publisher. That means you cant send me extras from your library. Not even from a bookstore. You must write to the publisher and order books sent direct. You might send me a machine gun hidden between the pages of a book.

There are lots of other rules. A year ago I made lists of all of them. Then i wrote notes next to each rule, giving reasons why the rule was stupid. i wanted to write letters to protest the stupidest ones, but my writing was so bad i knew they would only laugh at me. That was when i started going to the library to look up words. i wanted to write letters to the superintendent, the supervisor of corrections, the governor, and anyone else i could think of. For the first time in my life i found out the names of people with titles and power.

The first rule i protested was the one which said our outgoing letters must be left unsealed. At that time i didnt even have anyone to write to. But anyway. The authorities said our mail was not read, only held up to the light or felt to make sure no illegal contents were being sent

15

out (they never could tell me just what it would be possible for me to send out). i accused the authorities of lying, monitoring our mail in violation of their own policy and federal law. My letter was printed in the prison newspaper.

i never got an answer. i am sure the letters i sent to the governor and others never got out. But i got attention from the guards. i better not say what kind of attention or i might get more.

i found out that they *have* to send out legal communications— appeals, suits, etc. i started to read law books. i prepared a suit charging the California Adult Authority with tampering with the U.S. mails. i knew i would not get anywhere, but i did stir things up. They didn't change anything. But they noticed me. Troublemaker. They wont forget when i come up for parole again. i knew that when i started writing the letters and when i started the suit. But I had to do it. Why? The answer is very simple—to stay alive. Something in me knew i was fighting the death of my mind. With my instinct for self-preservation i started to protest the stupidity of this institution. Doing it made me less stupid. i started to think. i sharpened my mind. i studied books. i read. i wrote.

Isnt that rehabilitation? No. What i have done and what i continue to do only says i am a troublemaker. And troublemakers do not make parole. In order to make parole i would have to be dead. But i could not die. If i believed in god, like my mother does, i would say thank god i could not do what was necessary because then i would really be dead. i am still alive. Still a man. Which means they may decide to keep me longer and longer. Sometimes i wake up at night sweating, thinking i cant win and one way or another, they will kill me. They could legally keep me here as long as five years. It might as well be a death sentence.

You must think i exaggerate. It is easy to turn paranoid here. Am i insane? i know i am not. i know it every time a guard shows me i am right, and the guards (the Correctional Officers, they like to be called) are always showing me that I am right. The guards are prisoners here, just like me. Worse, because they will spend their whole lives here. i told that to a guard once, and he turned red, his eyes bulged, and he almost hit me. Then i knew i was right, and the guards are always fighting their own minds, trying not to know the truth about their lives. That is why they hate to be called guards. Then i knew i was much stronger than them because I face truth. This made me very dangerous to them and i can tell by the way they look at me that they would like to kill me. i watch them and try to understand their behavior. i study them like a scientist. i have written an article about them, but it is not publishable in the prison newspaper. And if i tried to send it out, there would be more trouble for me.

The other great truth i learned was that guards fear prisoners. Guards carry gossip, racial insults, lies. They do this because they are afraid of us and want to keep us hating each other. They try to trick us into behavior that puts us even more in their power and may hurt our chances of getting out. "Are you a communist?" one said to me last week when he threw my copy of the Free Weekly into my cell. i get only about every third issue, and when i ask about it, the guard laughs and says, "Oh, can you read?" Insults like that are as regular as cell checks, work calls, mess calls. Routine. But there are more of them when i am tired or feeling low. Like the guard knows when to trap me. One always picks the times i am reading to interrupt with an insult. i used to answer back. It took awhile for me to learn that he would take any casual answer i made and make it sould like grounds for punishment, like loss of privileges for a day or two. And his report goes into my file. Most interruptions come when i am writing. It must make them mad to see books by ex-cons on best seller lists. They must be afraid that some day i will be a famous writer while they are still stuck here.

So you see the kind of trap i am in. All these reports count against me when i come up for parole. Yet these things are the only sign that I am a man. The only way. No, not the only way. Now I have you too.

Enough. Maybe too much. But i have to say the truth, to you, to them too if this happens to be one of the letters they read.

For freedom,
Gary

P.S. i sent you a bunch of poems. i hope you like them.

Sunday
February 20

Dear Sally,

Its nearly two weeks since i wrote. Did my letter dated February 7 reach you? i read the carbon copy i keep, and i see many reasons why it might not get out. If that is what happened, i will renew my suit against the Adult Authority for tampering with the U.S. Mails.

Maybe you have decided you dont want to write to me. i understand. To get long, rambling, bitter letters and piles of bad poems in the mail is very boring.

Just inform me if you got the letter so that i know whether or not to proceed with another suit.

i have enjoyed our correspondence. Thank you.

Gary Wilson

2/22

Dear Gary,

Heavens no, I haven't abandoned you. Many things, including some concerning you directly, were keeping me busy. I got the letter of 2/7. I'll follow this note with a longer letter as soon as I can, tomorrow, or next day at the latest.

Love,

Sally

Thursday
Feb. 24

Dear Gary,

I was stricken when I read your note. My stupid imagination got in gear and I was able to glimpse what it must be like to have your life in the hands of irrational forces and capricious people, and to be dependent for outside contact on a muddle-headed woman who is so insensitive as to go along for ten days without answering your letter. My lapse seems unforgivable, though, to tell the truth, I've been falling into bed late each night and crawling out next morning with hardly a moment to spare. The trouble with being a "housewife" is that everyone assumes you've unlimited time for the co-op board and the Free Clinic rummage sale and so many other things that need doing, so how can I say no? On top of it all, since this is an election year, I'm committed to trying to keep our representative in congress.

18

It seems that no sooner is one election over than it's time to get ready for the next one, and most of my energy seems to go into just holding the line against losses of small gains won years ago.

Some personal problems (minor compared to yours) add to the strain, including my mother's imminent annual visit, which never stops shaking me up, before, during and after. (You were very astute to note that my parents didn't approve of some of the choices I've made in my life.) Enough of all that.

I've had several discussions with the lawyer I mentioned, and he told me that the situation you are in is by no means unusual. He gave me material to read on plea bargaining, how public defenders function with judges to get through crowded court calendars, processing cases like so many sticks of salami. I was simply outraged. But I suppose that again shows my naivete. I am always being outraged at what I learn about the way human beings treat each other. I should be unshockable by now!

My lawyer friend does not feel qualified to do much for you, but he did contact a group called People's Appeal, which specializes in cases like yours. Perhaps you already know about them. Anyway they will be in touch with you. In the meantime, he says, you should pursue the parole application, stressing the circumstances of your case. Several of the people in People's Appeal are old "marching buddies" of mine, from back in the days (it was only a few years ago, but seems like a lifetime) when we picketed and marched and afterward danced at fund-raising parties. (Now most of the people we knew then are divorced or ill or in rural communes or practicing meditation, and we're down to a very few friends whom we still see regularly.) I certainly will keep after them to do what they can for you.

I was impressed by your poetry. When you said you would send it, I expected a few sheets, not a great stack. Though I am not a reliable judge of literature, I must say I was shaken by the passion in every line. I hope you don't mind that I showed your poems to a friend, Dennis Powers, who teaches writing at Bay Junior College. I had already told him about you, and he was eager to see your poems when I told him about receiving them. Dennis used to be a poet, but he hasn't written anything for years. He is a fine teacher, and a very good, gentle person. He did not say very much as he read your poems, and he refused to respond to my demands that he say whether or not you were "good." He explained to me that questions of good or bad are the wrong questions now, that you are just starting out, and that you are in such a vulnerable and precarious state that all he could say to you would be, "Write on!" He says your best poems are the simple, angry ones in which your unique voice breaks through. He said, "Continue to simplify. And trust yourself." He did not want to say more, feeling it might be too soon to offer more criticism, but that if you wanted him to, you could write him in care of the college, and he would try to help.

Then he selected one, "Cell Sounds in Darkness," (is that the one that started as a list of things that were driving you crazy?) and suggested I take it up to Mary and Ives at the Free Weekly. It'll be in the next issue. So, as of the first of March, you'll be a PUBLISHED POET. I hope you're as pleased about that as I am. I used to write a little, and I remember the first time I saw a story of mine in print. Nothing equals the feeling, except, perhaps, seeing your child right after birth. (Now I only write hasty and scrappy letters, protesting the latest oil spill or urging amnesty for political prisoners.)

So, you see, I didn't forget you, but put off writing so that I would have some solid news for you. I didn't want to write, "I'm going to try this or that . . ." because so often people make promises they can't keep. I wanted to tell you, "I've *done* . . ." Something real instead of just rambling on about the trivia of my crowded life.

I used to call it a full life. Now it merely seems crowded. What's the difference? I asked Bob, and he (quite rightly) couldn't be bothered to take the time to answer. He is still the same vigorous, driving man he was when I met him, juggling many projects, loving them all, loving to be in motion. His only sign of age is a slight deafness developed during the past few years, and sometimes I think he is mostly deaf to silly, niggling questions like that. He said, "Eh?" patted me on the shoulder, then picked up the phone and went on making calls to remind people of the next teachers' union meeting.

I hope you've forgiven me now. If some days go by without your hearing from me, it will never, never mean I've dropped you to take up macrame or kung fu, though I can't blame you if you occasionally feel that people lucky enough to be on the outside fritter away their precious hours of free life.

Your friend,

Sally

P.S. Do you want the Free Weekly to print your poem under a pen name?

P.P.S. I'm very curious about your vegetarianism. Are you sure you're getting enough protein?

Saturday
February 26

Dear Sally,

i found your letter on the floor of my cell when i got back from working in the laundry. i read it over and over before i went to sleep last night. And this morning, during my first free time, I sit down to begin my answer. i can answer you right away because i have the time. You do not have time hanging on you like a weight. ive been unfair to expect you to answer my letters as fast as i answered yours. From now on i will remember what you said—if you do not write, you have not forgotten me. i will remember that other people make demands on you because you can be depended on to help them when they are in need. i hope you will not mind if i go on writing long letters pouring out the things i cant say to anyone here, and then waiting impatiently for your next letter. i have better understanding now, but i still have no patience.

Tell the Free Weekly they can use my real name. i wonder what it will feel like to see my deep feelings in print. Does the Free Weekly pay much? I cant receive money. They can deposit money in my canteen account. i can use it to buy cigarettes and nuts. Tell Dennis I appreciate his advice. i intend to send him some poems and ask for more help in finding my "unique voice."

i bought some jars of nuts and some peanut butter with the money you sent.

Yes, good nutrition is a problem in a place like this. One of the subjects i began to study when i started reading was nutrition. i learned that one does not need flesh to survive, so i stopped eating flesh. There are many reasons for this, but the one that is strongest is the killing of the innocent. That is the law of the world, from the killing of innocent animals to the killing of prisoners. But i am not a pacifist. Life has taught me that i must fight to stay alive. But i do not want to fight blindly anymore. I do not want to fight myself. I want to find the true enemy and destroy him. That is why i no longer eat the corpses of murdered animals. Whatever fight is in me, whatever anger is in me, i want to save, store up for the fight against the exploiters, the killers.

Yes, i heard of Peoples Appeal but i never got in touch with them. I used only my own efforts, "a jailhouse lawyer," protesting alone. i was proud of being a loner. But now i think you have shown me it is wise to reach out to grasp the helping hand that is offered. (Some day i may tell you how hard it was for me to answer your Christmas card with a letter—to confess i needed someone.) As soon as i hear from Peoples Appeal i will send them all documents, including the preliminary things i have done for my next parole application.

There is another reason why i want the Free Weekly to use my name when they print the poem. That poem is not as political as many of my others are, so i do not think it can do me any harm, except for the harm of being printed in a "subversive sheet" like the Free Weekly. It should qualify as evidence of "constructive, rehabilitative activity." The parole board would be impressed that ive written something good enough to get published. They would have to take my writing seriously, the way your friend Dennis does.

I am preparing my parole application now. So far i have a good work record, no complaints from work supervisors, so that may offset the times i have been on report for debating with guards. i doubt i can get a hearing before fall. The Parole Board meets for a few hours each time. They squeeze in many applications, with only a few minutes for each. They will interview me, but thats only another minute or two. So you see why i need some good, short bits of "rehabilitation" like fast TV commercials that sock them with the message to "buy" me. So i will clip my poem from the Free Weekly and have it put into my file.

Maybe i will make my living writing when i get out of here. i have a lot to say, so many things stored up from my whole life. Things about my childhood. Things i have seen here that i cant tell in letters, that sometimes seem unbelievable, even to me.

Sometimes i think i am not in a prison but in an insane asylum that is run to drive the patients mad, not to cure them. Once i read about experiments on mice, where things were done to drive the mice crazy, and the scientists wrote up papers telling which things worked fastest and how long it took to drive a mouse crazy. i feel like one of those mice. And then i think that a society that would have places like this must be crazy, the whole society stark, raving mad, and putting men in places like this to drive us madder. And if a man hopes for anything, it is easier for them to drive him mad. So i never let myself hope.

Now you have come to offer hope. And to tell the truth, that scares me.

Do you have a picture of yourself? I would like to put it on the wall of my cell. Yes, they do let us put things on the wall (though by tomorrow someone could invent a stupid rule about that too). Then, when i get shaky, i can look up and see my friend Sally.

Peace,

Gary

Wed. March 1

Dear Gary,

I'm sorry, I should have made it clear that Free Weekly pays nothing for anything it publishes and, in fact, only barely manages to keep going with donations and benefit parties. (I'm so sick of benefit parties that now I only buy tickets on the condition that I needn't go.) I hope this doesn't spoil your pleasure at being published, but I think you'll find that most papers or magazines which would be interested in publishing unknown, controversial poets can't afford to pay. So, although I don't want to throw cold water on your plans and hopes, I don't think you should expect to be able to earn a living by writing. Even established writers seldom earn enough by writing to live. That's why so many of them, like Dennis, teach creative writing in colleges. The problem will be to find you something to do that supports you but leaves you enough time and energy to write. I asked Dennis about it, and he sighed and said he knew of no serious writer who had solved this problem short of marrying money or inheriting it.

What you said about prison as an insane asylum was confirmed by another friend of mine, the only one I know who has done time (except overnight after demonstrations). I hope you don't mind that I showed him that part of your letter. I wanted him to help me understand better what you are living day after day. (I also showed him the part about your vegetarianism, since, although he is not a vegetarian, he is a pacifist.)

I met Sam Jones several years ago on a picket line in front of the Oakland Draft Board, and we have been good friends ever since. Sam was about your age when World War II began. He declared himself a conscientious objector and refused to be drafted. It's hard for anyone who was not alive at that time to imagine what this meant. A person your age has never known what it meant to live in a country which was sure of its virtue and good purpose. Certainly I remember how I felt—we were going to make the world safe for democracy, and I left school to help make the bombs we were told would do so. We believed that anyone who saw that war in any other way was a traitor or a fool. (Some people, even liberals, still feel this way. There's a certain coolness between Sam and some other friends of mine, a Jewish couple.)

Sam was put into a camp for conscientious objectors, where he spent two years, and then two years more at a federal prison. What he says about the prison matches what you have said, except that prisons were in some ways much worse in those days. He could receive only tiny amounts of mail, and no books or newspapers at all. There was nothing to read but a few tattered books wheeled around from cell to cell in a small box. His letters were openly and rigidly censored; writing anything about his daily life in prison was forbidden, as were so many other subjects that, he says, writing a letter was a near impossibility.

It was, Sam says, like living among unstable people being pushed to the point of lunacy, under a regime designed to play upon every weakness of a man and drive him to desperate violence. When I asked him how he came out of it the gentle person he is, he said that any violent urges had left him long before, when he was only a boy. He lost his temper and struck at another boy with his hunting knife (I can't imagine it, but Sam swears it happened) and narrowly missed. From that time on, "I was never angry again." It's true. Sam is a man literally incapable of anger.

When the war ended, he was paroled to Berkeley. He had no money, and, as a convicted felon, he was barred from most of the jobs available. (He could not even vote. The law has just been changed, and Sam says that this November, at the age of fifty-three, he expects to vote for the first time.) He earned money mowing lawns, cleaning basements, things like that. Later he learned carpentry and now he has his own building business (mostly a one-man operation). He was never able to afford any formal education, but has read more than most of the university graduates I know (and discusses his reading with a humility they often lack!)

If you saw Sam, you would probably not be impressed. He is short (not more than an inch or two taller than I, which is very short for a man) thin, almost fragile looking (though he is really very strong). He looks much younger than he is, hardly more than forty. He is very quiet, and, when he does speak, seems hesitant. But his voice is very clear and pure. I love to hear him speak; his voice makes me think of pure, clear, transparent water.

I am sending you a picture of me, taken on the campus last week by a stranger in a hurry who kept frowning suspiciously as if he wondered what respectable woman would be out with a camera at six-thirty in the morning. He moved the camera, but through the blur you can see me, muffled up in my coat, my hair (I'd given myself a too hasty haircut the night before) blown up spiky as if my head comes to a point (it really doesn't!) But at least Yossarian came out all right. He is looking after a stick I threw, considering whether or not he will indulge me by retrieving it. (He finally decided not to bother.) I took pictures all along the way as Yossarian and I took our favorite early morning walk. But it was too dark, so none of the others came out. Another of my good ideas come to nothing. But I can give you a word picture of our walk.

Crown Court comes down into Spruce Street, which winds all the way from the very top of the hill (way up beyond our place) down to the campus. There's not much traffic at five in the morning, and most of the houses are hidden uphill behind trees and shrubs, so it's like running down a wooded mountain. Don't you love downhill walks, gravity pulling at you to hurry you forward, as if promising you something below, urging you to it!

Spruce ends at one corner of the campus, and Yossarian goes wild (for about two minutes, then remembers his dignity) as we enter the campus, where he can run freely at this time of day. It is still and lovely, with the light just beginning to come to the sky behind the high hills, tall trees, tall buildings, like castles in an enchanted forest. I cross bridges over creeks and know that at this hour of the morning there must be trolls under the bridges. And the campanile points straight up, high above everything, a magic tower with a great eye watching us wander up toward Sproul Plaza, which is empty except for the leaves and papers blown by the wind.

25

We come out on Telegraph Avenue as a few shopkeepers are washing their windows or hosing down the sidewalks. It's all fresh and clean there now and looks like a charming old-fashioned street of shops and cafes. There's a bookstore on one corner where the owner knows me, and when he sees me coming he invites me in to share coffee he brews on a hot plate in the back. He tells me about new books coming out and reads his own poetry to me.

I wish you could take this walk with me. Some day you will. I suppose it's impossible for me to get a picture of you. What about a word picture?

Love,

Sally

Saturday
March 4

Dear Sally,

Your letter and the Free Weekly arrive together. The (inmate) librarian saw my poem printed in the Free Weekly. He showed me an old copy of WRITERS MARKET and GUIDE TO ALTERNATIVE PRESSES. I would like to send some of my poems to publishers on those lists if i do not run out of money for postage too soon. The trouble is that i must pay for postage and the envelope both ways (some of my poems might be returned). At 17 cents an hour, it takes many hours of work in the plate plant to pay for a few envelopes and stamps.

No, that is not a misprint. 17¢—seventeen cents—$.17 per hour. For what kind of work? Making license plates or furniture. The furniture shop is the best place, where desks and chairs are made for schools and libraries. Everyone wants to work there. I have never worked there because i have been put down as a troublemaker. Laundry, kitchen, maintenance and all outdoor work is unpaid.

But this place is called a farm. What about all that healthy outdoor work? i thought that i would like hoeing rows of potatoes, but i dont. Its that lousy 17 cents an hour, turning us into slaves who produce license plates and furniture that ought to be made by free men at a decent wage. i will come out of here with one skill—making plates— which are made only in prisons. So i am in conflict. i want to work to

26

pass the time and to make a good report that will get me out of here. Yet, the man inside me rebels against being exploited.

You were right about the feeling of seeing my poem in print. I feel high and inspired to write more and more. I think i will soon have another stack of poems to send to you, and maybe to Dennis.

Your friend Sam Jones must be a fine man. I am surprised he has stayed alive so long. i never knew anyone like him. If i had, i might not be here now. i hope that i will be able to do something like him when i leave this place. My main skills are in cabinetry, not rough carpentry, though ive done both. Being sent here lost my apprentice status in the union. (was laid off anyway) i too would like to set up my own business when i am out, but parole will not allow that. A mans individual efforts are nothing. He has to have a job working for someone else. There are agencies that get jobs for parolees, jobs no self-respecting man wants. Non-union, minimum wage. The same slave labor as here. But i will take any job to get my freedom. Once out i can look for something else. i hear that unemployment is worse than ever. You probably read the Free Weekly article on the cut-backs in welfare and unemployment insurance. i am glad my mother lives in a rich mans house and will not go hungry. She will want to make a home for me again when i come out, but i won't let her. She is old, and i should be taking care of her. i cant do that yet, but at least i can make sure i will be no burden on her. And some day i will be able to do more for her.

i called my mother old, but she is not much older than you. In your picture you look like a little blond Dutch girl (i like your haircut). My mother is a big woman and heavy from eating cheap starchy food all her life. She has high blood pressure and bad knees, probably arthritis, and her hair is almost white. When i compare her picture to yours, i think she could be your mother. i once saw a picture of her taken when she was sixteen. She was tall and slim with thick red hair and she was laughing. i almost never saw her laugh because she was ashamed to show her bad teeth, which are all gone now—she had false teeth since she was forty. i guess she didnt have much to laugh at anyway.

i like reading about your family and friends. i would tell you about my friends, but i dont have any. None of the people i knew were much at writing. But even before i was sent here, i was never really close to them. We drove and drank together, but i dont think we ever really talked. We got together to forget things, not to face them or talk about

27

them. i dont know what happened to the people i used to know. It is like i have been dropped into a dark hole and forgotten. Now i am just another of the sad things they try to forget when they get together for a drink. So i try not to think of them. i would rather think about you, about your friend Sam, about your husband Bob, who started poor like me, but who won—with the help of a fantastic woman. What does he look like?

I will try to give you a word picture of me. i am tall, nearly six feet four inches. i have blue eyes and straight dirty-blonde hair. i am thin—my waist is thirty inches. i have always been thin no matter how much i eat. My skin is very white (like my mothers). Teachers always said i looked sickly because of my thin body and pale skin, but thats just the way i am. i never get suntanned. i just get red, then fade to white again. i get very red when i am mad.

In other words i am a WASP—white, anglo-saxon, protestant (atheist but my mother is a Baptist). What a joke. i am a WASP, the rich and powerful class in this country. i do not belong to any of the oppressed groups that all the books are written about. Sometimes i wonder if i exist at all.

But I look at my poem in the Free Weekly, and I feel solid and real, all six feet four of me. They have heard from me now, and they will hear a lot more.

Your poet,

Gary

Sat. 3/11

Dear Gary,

I am stiff in every joint and feel, not like the "little Dutch girl" you saw in the photo (my, it *was* foggy—and that hair is much more gray than blonde) but like an ancient crone who may never move again. I'd been kept away from the garden by so many things that I knew we would not have a garden at all this summer, unless I did something fast. So today I tried to make up for lost time. Like Willy Loman, I feel lost unless I've got "something in the ground." I grow vegetables on narrow little terraces up and down the side of the hill, wherever the trees don't block out sun completely, a most awkward way to garden. But awkwardness, aches and pains and all, I love it. I got in a row of radishes, at least, and they should be pushing up out of the ground at about the same time my muscles stop screaming their out-rage.

The envelopes and stamps should have arrived by now. I'll send that many the first of every month. Let me know if you need more. I sent $10 to be deposited in your canteen account, and you can count on that every month too. I wish it could be more.

I spoke to Sam about your carpentry skills. He would like to be able to promise the parole board a steady job for you, but he usually takes only as much work as he can handle himself, which he says is the only way he can survive. As soon as he has a steady payroll to meet, he begins to lose money, and he has heavy responsibilities: a wife and two children, plus two more children and alimony from a previous marriage.

Bob is just under six feet and quite heavily built, not fat but broad. His face is freckled and he has a typically Irish pug nose. There is a scar on his chin from a fight (one of the many fights of his childhood). He used to have sandy hair but is quite bald now. Despite his baldness he looks young. He is very gregarious, can talk to anyone, and in five minutes get their commitment to join a group or serve on a committee. He is still a fighter, at his best when someone challenges him, tries to thwart him. Then he seems to gather all his forces and start a whole movement to get his way. He never has been afflicted by the doubts that have slowed me down lately, never looks twice at a defeat, but goes right on. He has migraine headaches which put him out of it a couple days a month, but as soon as he recovers he is right back in the middle of six campaigns.

When Bob and I first met, I didn't like him at all. I think we fell in love in the midst of an argument in a coffee shop on Telegraph Avenue (since replaced by a book shop, then by a rather cutsy art-craft shop). Bob was talking about the use of a university education, which (of course, considering his background) he saw as a road to making money. He talked about how his sociology major and psych minor would lead him to a career in advertising. I was full of socialist rhetoric from my shipyard days, and I poured it all on him. I believe I finished by calling him a traitor to the working class he belonged to and quoted something from Shakespeare, on men who climb the ladder of power and never look back at those people who are on the rungs below. (I've always been an awful blabbermouth.)

29

I thought he would get up and leave. But his eyes gleamed at the prospect of a good fight. We left the coffee shop and wandered around the dark, empty campus, shouting at one another. Neither of us noticed the time until, suddenly, it seemed less dark and we saw the glimmer of sunrise and realized we'd walked and talked all night.

By that time Bob was converted. He would be a teacher instead of an advertising tycoon, a public school teacher who would help youngsters near the age he was when he had left school. Within a couple of months I left school and we were married.

Bob started teaching in Berkeley in 1955 in an all black junior high school. He immediately became an organizer for the teachers' union (still risky in those days) and a campaigner for school integration. By the time bussing started he was already working on other innovative programs. (Last year he didn't teach but worked on proposals for federal grants.) He's now teaching in one of the experimental schools, but funds are running short and things at the school are pretty disorganized—I recognize his restlessness. He says he may take a sabbatical next year to work on some other project.

In our dining room there's an old, round oak table I found at the dump back in 1949, and it seems to me that through the years there've been more meetings than meals at that table. We're always clearing off one project to make room for another. I wish I had a penny for each cup of coffee I've poured! Sometimes I come home to find a group sitting around the table without Bob—he's run off to attend another meeting!

If you had encountered someone like Bob at your junior high school, things might have turned out differently for you. But who can say? Our son John had daily contact with him, but left school during his second year of high school. I defended him, insisting we had to give him a chance to try to find his way by other means. Since he was sixteen, John has been off on his own for long periods, once in a commune, then at odd jobs in the valley, twice in Mexico, once to Europe, briefly in Canada. Between sorties in search of himself, John turns up at home again. I think I told you he has recently returned. He's talking about trying school again, Bay Junior College (where Dennis teaches).

You must be very conscious, as I am, of the similarity between your situation and my son's. The difference being that with the cushion of a middle class home, John was free to explore deviant ways of existence with both financial and psychological support from us (though Bob has become rather grudging with both). It seems quite clear that had John displayed these feelings and behavior in a setting like the one you grew up in, his situation now might be different.

Even my fingers are beginning to ache, though I look at the dirt under the nails with some satisfaction. I must get some sleep.

Love,

Sally

P.S. I was very touched by your devotion to your mother. I'm sure you'll do much to make her proud of you in the future.

P.P.S. I wanted to write a letter protesting the work situation you describe, but I'm afraid I might do you more harm than good. Tell me if you want me to.

Wednesday
March 15

Dear Sally,

I have just been released from Adjustment (solitary) where i spent three days for taking some extra fruit from the kitchen. With plenty of time to think, i conclude that i was really being punished for writing some of my opinions in my letters to you. Though i have not written one tenth of what i know and see and feel, i believe i have already written far too much. i must follow the rule your friend Sam lived under—not to mention anything about what happens here.

i have sent you a present i finished making in Adjustment. i hope you like it.

So you are a gardener too. i remember when we were in the Army Street project i begged my mother for seeds to plant a garden. She finally bought me a little package of sunflower seeds and i planted them across the front of our building. Soon they came up. Twelve of them survived and grew taller and taller. i was only six at the time, and i was proud but a little scared that i had made these flowers grow taller and taller. i watered them every day. The flowers opened up like twelve faces of friendly giants bending their heads to look down at me.

Then some kids, i guess, decided to have some fun. Each day when i got up i would find one flower chopped off. i tried to stay up at night

31

and watch to see who was doing it, but i always fell asleep, then woke up to find another headless stalk. They weren't even stealing them for the seeds—i always found the head thrown on the ground a few feet away. In 12 days all my sunflowers were decapitated. i cried the first three days, but after that i did not cry. i just kept asking my mother, why?

Later i understood vandalism. Or i should say i practised it. Without understanding, without wanting to understand anything anymore. Now when i look back on the windows i broke and the bus seats i slashed i remember how i felt while i was doing it, how the sight of anything clean or fresh or new made me want to destroy. The world is full of people who feel the way i did. Because something inside them has been hurt they hate anything hopeful like my sunflowers. Wrecking and killing is a way of saying, "i am here, see my mark." It is what people do when they see no other way of making a mark on the world, when they are nothing.

i studied tree pruning when i was in the Job Corps (another kind of prison set up so the local businesses can get government money). i have often thought that if there is no work for me in any of the building trades, i would always be able to earn enough to get by in gardening. That might mean living somewhere outside of San Francisco, in a place where there are more gardens. i doubt the parole board would let me go back to SF anyway.

We are allowed private gardens here, but i have no seeds. Could you send me some? If i am to get any food worth eating, i think i must grow it myself. Just two or three things i can eat raw. Maybe even some flowers to look at. Not sunflowers.

Love,

Gary

Mon. March 20

Dear Gary,

I was so furious when I heard about your being put in solitary confinement that I telephoned the superintendent, person to person, and asked (in as icy a tone as I could) why such a harsh punishment should be given for taking an extra portion of fruit. I asked if you were possibly being persecuted for something else.

He said something ridiculous about your using fruit to make liquor, as if you could operate a still in a 6 × 8 cell! I would have said more, but by that time I was beginning to be afraid I might have made things even worse for you, so I just told him I was interested in your welfare and hung up. Now I'm stricken with shame and fear, feeling I probably did the wrong thing and will only bring on more reprisals or even delay the time when you will be released. I hope you can forgive me.

I've sent an assortment of seeds.

The purse arrived. I don't know what to say. At first I was simply filled with pleasure looking at the delicate, shiny weave. All I thought about was how thoughtful you were to send it and I wondered where and how you could have gotten it. It took some time before I realized (it was John who first spotted the design) that it was made from cigarette packages.

When I realized that, I sat down and cried. I thought of you sitting in your cell, collecting, folding, weaving hundreds and hundreds of cigarette packages into this beautiful form. I know it is impossible for anyone outside to imagine what it is like to be locked up day after day, but for a moment, I think, I had a bare glimpse of what your life is like. Then I felt all the more miserable at the thought that I might have done anything to prolong your agony, when truly I only hope to alleviate and shorten it.

Must stop. Two meetings going on upstairs (I'm in the dungeon and they keep calling for me) and a call from my mother proposing a visit. The meetings go on very late, and I awaken early in the morning, so my sleep is cut off at both ends.

Love,
Sally

Wednesday
March 22

Dear Sally,

You are a wonderful, beautiful person. You feel things. You could never do me harm.

33

The superintendent was not all the way off base. There are things men do to prove they are men. i cant explain. Others are involved. But im pretty sure your phone call did me no harm. It might even do some good, showing that someone on the outside cares enough to make a long distance call.

I am glad you liked the purse, but sorry that it made you cry. i cant tell you how many hours it took. i started it when you first wrote to me. It went faster than the first one which i made for my mother. i am glad it made you understand a little more of my life here. Not that i want you to suffer with me, but i feel we are closer because you understand more, closer because you cried for me. i dont think anyone has cried for me for a long time.

It is true that people on the outside who take an interest in prisoners often do no good. Since the Attica Prison revolt it has become fashionable for liberals to write to prisoners, to help them. But what real help can they give? The best help is to try to get a man out. This goes much farther than most people are willing to go. What they do instead is write letters full of revolutionary rhetoric, making the prisoner an object of suspicion to the authorities. Or they get naive and ignorant prisoners to act with defiance. Then they find a new fad and drop him, leaving him in worse shape than before, identified as a "radical" but with no protection from outside. I was warned not to answer your Christmas card, not to get mixed up with any liberals who would "mouth off" and then forget me. i was suspicious of you at first. But your description of Yossarian made me decide to take a chance on you. i thought a woman who felt that way about her dog and even about her turtles wouldnt let me down. And i know i was right.

The best thing a prisoner can have is someone on the outside who cares and has strength and energy to back it up. It affects those in power, and it affects the parole board. For instance, if your friend Dennis were to put his reaction to my poetry in writing, and i could have a copy put into my file for the parole board, it might help. Any sign that a person on the outside thinks a prisoner is worth something. Do you think he would be offended if i asked him to write something? Just something short, not to take up his valuable time.

i have been reading a lot of modern war poetry. It is surprising how similar the emotions are between the men at war and prisoners here. i am starting to write a series of poems showing those similarities.

How long does it take these magazines to make up their minds? i guess i expected to hear right away, but someone told me at least six weeks before i hear anything and then months to get it in print. If thats true, prison has prepared me very well for the life of a writer— waiting—doing time.

Love,

Gary

P.S. Twice you have mentioned not sleeping well. Is there something wrong? If so you should share it with me. Not that i could help. But i can care.

Thurs. 3/20

Dear Gary,

Dennis has written a short, businesslike statement about your writing, as follows:

I have read a large sampling of the poetry of Gary Wilson. While somewhat derivative (as is normal in the work of young writers) it contains strong images and explores serious themes. It seems to me the work of a serious writer and compares favorably with work turned in to me in my creative writing classes at Bay Junior College.

I've given a copy of it to People's Appeal (which I understand is helping you get your parole material together) and sent one to the Cal. Adult Authority. I've also been trying to get an interview with a Mr. Agtente, of the C.A.A. to talk about your case, but so far my letters haven't been answered. Is there anyone else Dennis or I should write to? Is there anyone else I should contact to say I have a *steady and permanent* interest in your welfare?

I'm sorry that some of my private problems crept in and affected the tone of my last letter. I didn't intend that. It's true that for the past year or so my sleep has been poor and short. I'm always awake before dawn. I used to be awakened by a recurring nightmare. Do you remember the poster carried in some peace marches of the late sixties? that of a mutilated Vietnamese child, half her face blown open like a mouth gaping into her skull? That child haunted my dreams and woke me with a sense of horror, guilt and impotency, not only about the war, but about the suffering in general which is the lot of most human beings. In some dreams her awful mouth screamed in pain while I listened helplessly, and woke trembling and supine, my position symbolic of my ineffectuality. I knew I should simply do all I could, then put it aside at night and sleep. But nothing I did seemed to hold back the sense of futility that began to creep over me, I'm not sure just when, the feeling that it was all meaningless motion. (Bob has little patience with such doubts, and his deafness increases if I voice them.)

Do you really want to hear about this? I keep feeling that making a complaint to you about my life is a form of indecent exposure.

A more concrete if minor problem is that my mother plans to visit us in April or May. You were right when you inferred that my parents did not approve of some choices I have made. My mother's disapproval is as fresh as it was thirty years ago, maybe stronger. When my father died, she moved to southern California where she must be lonely and bitter. This takes the form of her writing very reactionary political opinions which she must have picked up there—she was not always a bigot, though she disagreed with me. Bob insists on reading her letters aloud for laughs, and I guess that's the only way to read them without crying. Unhappy in her lonely life, she seems to need someone or something to blame. Lately she blames me. I can understand that her thinking is illogical and irrational, but that doesn't make me rational about her. When she comes to visit, as she does for a few weeks every year, we can't find any safe topics to talk about, and I am made tense and nervous by her sitting tight-lipped and disapproving.

There, now that I've written you about it, the problem doesn't seem so bad. In fact, as I might have predicted, I'm thoroughly ashamed of complaining about my mother's visit when I'm sure you'd give a great deal to be able to enjoy a long visit from your mother, or would probably not care who came to stay in your house if you had a house to live in and were free.

Forgive me,

Sally

Dear Sally,

Your letter was beautiful! You treated me like your real friend, not like a low-down person, a convict, a loser you felt sorry for and wanted to cheer up. When you wrote about your nightmare, about your mother, it was as if you put out your hand, not only to help me, but to take help from me in return. You treated me as an equal, as a friend. Never be afraid to tell me your troubles as i tell you mine. I am glad you need me as a friend, not the way i need you because you have a full, free life and many people who love you, but still in a special way, as a person you can trust.

I am a very proud person. My mother believes that pride is a sin, but without my pride i would have had nothing left. Each time i hear from you, i am happy, but also, the stiff pride in me asks, "How does she really feel about me? Why is she doing all this? What is in it for her?" I admit that all my life, whenever anyone tried to help me (i will not say no one did. There were teachers, a social worker when we were on welfare, a couple of guys in the Job Corps, a carpenter i worked for) i always wondered, "Whats in it for them?" i always felt like they must be using me.

Now i will tell you something you wont want to believe because you are so idealistic. I was right about all of them. They wanted to help me, but not just for myself. They wanted to mold me into something they could feel proud of. They wanted to say to themselves, "I took that no-good bum and made this or that out of him." And when i would not let them make me into what they thought i should be, they dropped me. They all stood up on a pedestal, reaching down to me, and the first time i did not do what they wanted, they said they had tried but i was hopeless.

But you do not stand on a pedestal and reach down. Your feet are on the earth with me. Your eyes look straight into mine. You reach out to me as a human being, offering me friendship. You ask from me, in return, friendship and comfort.

The reason you cant sleep is that you dont fool yourself the way liberals do. Elections, marches, meetings, what have they done? People are still dying in wars and still dying in prison and still dying on the streets. Those who are not dying have ways of forgetting the ones who are. One of those ways is liberal politics. But you are one of the rare people who cant forget.

i am usually awake before dawn too. Sometimes i wake up, not really awake, but just starting to come out of a dream. (In all my dreams I am free, outside.) Waking up, i do not remember where i am. i think i am in my own bed in the old project and the clatter i hear is my mother in the kitchen making my breakfast. Then i remember. Then a nightmare shiver comes over me, then terrible sadness, like the horror and sadness you feel when you dream of the mutilated child.

Do you believe in ESP? Next time I awake in the dark I will try to send my thoughts out to you. If you are asleep I will try to make them soothe you and keep you asleep. If you are awake, I will be with you. You try it too (even if you dont believe in ESP) and then both of us will know, when we wake up in the dark, that we are not alone.

I think the statement Dennis wrote is sure to help me. i wrote to thank him. i dont think that man from the adult authority will see you, but just writing letters to ask for an appointment shows youre interested, and that will help too.

i have another problem. i told you getting books here is a hassel? They must come direct from the publisher. i cant afford many so a few months ago i started writing to publishers to see if i could get free copies. Some wrote saying they would send free copies. The books never came. When i wrote a form query to the superintendents office, i was told that books must be bought, ordered through the canteen. In other words, that i cant receive books free from the publisher.

There is no such rule! The reason is something else. A lot of books get held up for strange reasons, and some cant get in at all because they are considered too radical. It just so happens that leftwing publishers are the ones most likely to send free copies. I told this to the lawyer from Peoples Appeal when he was here last week, and he thought i might have grounds for another suit against the prison, but it might not be wise to start something like that when i will be coming before the parole board in a few months. i might suddenly find myself on report for all kinds of little things.

Keeping books from me is like keeping food from me. i thought id never say that. i was never a great reader, and maybe i read a lot now because there is nothing else to do. No, thats not the only reason. Its the pressure of being here, pressure that squeezes a man down, compresses his life, activates his mind—the only means of survival. i look around me and see men dying day by day in different ways. If i were out on a battlefield i might run for my life. Here i must read for my life.

Love,
Gary

Dear Gary,

This note must be short, a million things pressing, including "domestic strife," Bob and John getting on each other's nerves. I spend a lot of time down in the dungeon just to get away from their quarrels. Bob, the ambitious lower-class boy, can't get over having raised a middle-class son.

And some sad news. Sam called to give us his new address (a room attached to a shed he rents to store tools) and phone number. He and his wife have separated. This was his second marriage. His first ended just about the time I met him. Both times, he admits, the separation was not his idea. How could anyone not want to be married to Sam? He is so good. Bob says, "Maybe too good," and points out a similarity between his two wives: both very emotional, unstable, needing "rescue," says Bob, "and marriage is not a rescue operation." I told him that if they needed rescue, that was all the more reason they should have stayed with Sam, but Bob shook his head and said, "People can never forgive anyone who rescues them." Then he added, "Nor a man who is incapable of anger." I don't know. All I know is now Sam is living in a little box, working night and day to support two families (two children in each) without the slightest sign of anger or self-pity at his plight. Maybe he *is* too good.

More soon.

Love,
Sally

P.S. Do you think political prisoners, like Sam, have any effect on prisons?

Dear Sally,

What happened?! All of a sudden theres a pile of books in my cell, with old postmarks. Someone broke the bottleneck and that some-one could only be you. Youre a miracle. I tell you about something and you dont say a word; you just do things. If there were more people like you in the world, it would be a different place. Maybe even i would be different. Tell me how you made this miracle.

I have thought alot about political prisoners like Sam. One day i talked with a man (burglar) who is pretty old and had been inside six prisons over the past forty years. He told me everything is different now from when he first did time. Not the prisons, but the thoughts of prisoners. Prisons, he says, are like the outside, only moreso. For instance in the fifties, political prisoners suffered because all the other prisoners were anti-communist like the rest of the country, and someone convicted of perjury in a political trial was lower than a rapist and had a bad time. But near the end of the fifties that started to change. The first draft resisters he saw coming in were different from the other prisoners. He says they started the big change. Just seeing a man who looked proud of what he was and what he had done—not phony proud but with real manly pride. Try to understand what that means. No one feels like a man anymore after that door locks shut behind him. The political prisoners of the early sixties, this old man said, "...were the only men who really knew why they were here."

Now that is a profound statement. I didnt know why i was here when i came. I knew the reasons the court said, but those werent the real reasons i was here. In here i learned more about the society that put me here, more about why i was so angry, why i ended up here.

Strange. Here in prison, only in the last few months, I learned that I am worth something, a precious human life that almost was lost. It was not meant to be taught by the prison. The intention of prison is the opposite. It magnifies and intensifies the process that put me here. In this magnification, did it make itself so large that I could finally recognize it, see it for what it really was? Or are the new thoughts on the outside magnified and intensified in here? It is hard to say exactly what is happening, but, yes, i would say political prisoners are part of it.

Of all oppressed people, the prisoner is the most oppressed. By being suddenly made a member of the most oppressed group in our society i was made conscious of my life-long oppression.

Love,
Gary

P.S. Am i starting to use too many long words again? i seemed to need them for what i was thinking. Well, i looked them all up and at least theyre spelled right.

Friday
April 21

Dear Gary,

Sorry I took so long to answer. More difficult things happening with friends, needs that couldn't wait.

Your letter was beautiful, your choice of words just right, your eloquence . . . well, I have nothing to teach *you* about writing.

It was no miracle. All I did was to write to the head of the Adult Authority, then to my state assemblyman and my representative in congress (both of whom have been in my home at benefit parties for their campaigns) all the daily papers in this area and two near the prison (none of which printed my letter), the governor and, of course, the Free Weekly, which printed my letter in the April 15 issue and promises to do a feature article on the problems of prisoners getting books, writing materials, etc. and will analyze the complicated and inconsistent regulations. Since the holding up of your books was a capricious act, not backed up by any rule, the likelihood is that the bottle-neck is only temporarily broken, so we may have to go through something like this again. But I cut my political teeth on bureaucratic tangles. The routine is pretty standard; one just has to write politely, firmly, persistently, in effect make a perfect pest of oneself, and, if possible, get into print somewhere, anywhere. I have become known as a persistent pest in the East Bay, and a politician once told me he would do anything he could to get me off his back. (He wasn't smiling.) This was a simple one—I wish they were all as easy. I can only conclude that you're right, it rarely happens that anyone protests a violation of a prisoner's rights, and a voice from outside is effective.

And the difficult things? I was going to skip over this part, but you don't want me to. Friends' troubles—they seem to come in bunches.

A friend attempted suicide last week. She is younger than I, about forty. A very attractive, bright woman who was divorced about a year ago after a good twenty year marriage. (Bob and I have calculated that now there is only one couple left, still married, of those we knew twenty years ago, when we were all young families, and that couple was the one we thought least likely to stay married—quarreling constantly but welded together like a Strindberg couple.)

I thought Barbara was enjoying her new life. She looked young, prettier than ever. She was free of children (one daughter married, the other off to college) and went to live in a commune with nine young people. She was active in politics, the women's movement, was studying yoga, dance, painting. I admired Barbara and sometimes I envied her.

Last week she took an overdose of sleeping pills. I didn't even know she was taking pills for sleep. She didn't empty the whole bottle, and she doesn't seem to be very clear on what she had done or why. "I was tired, so tired, I needed a good long sleep." There was something about a much younger man she was involved with, but I don't think that was the real reason. I think she was telling the truth, that she was just tired, tired because her attempts to create a new life for herself are exhausting. I feel guilty and sorry that those of us who can rest on the cushion of traditional patterns just weren't giving her the kind of support she needed. Bob and I got into a silly argument about her, and I accused him of feeling just a twinge of satisfaction that she wasn't quite making it as she pretended to. Bob admitted he did slightly resent a woman who seemed to be getting on well without a man. (Which is doubly unfair, since Barbara's husband left her for a much younger woman, then settled into a comfortable marriage identical to the one he had with Barbara. His new wife even looks like Barbara!)

She is still in a daze, as if the sleeping pills continue to take effect, though the doctor says that can't be true. He says she must not be alone for a few days. I invited her to stay in my daughter's old room for a week or two. Mostly she lies there, still, while my son plays loud records in the room next door. I offered to make him turn down the volume, but she said she likes to "feel the vibration" of the music. I wish I knew what to do for her.

Happier news. I have become a grandmother. My daughter and her husband live in Mass so I'm rather a long-distance grandmother. Nancy married a physicist who works for various corporations on a series of vague projects. I suspect they are vague, so far as we are concerned, because they must be Defense Department-financed, and Nancy knows I would disapprove. I wanted to be with her when she had the baby (a boy) but she was very independent about it, insisting that I stay home and carry on with "your usual frantic round of good causes." I'm sure she didn't mean that to sound as condescending as it does. We're both very careful not to criticize each other's values, which, as you can see, are too far apart to bear talking about.

I've examined my feelings about being so far from my grandchild and decided that the deprivation is not vital. I'd love to cuddle the baby and walk him in the park, but I won't die from the lack. Mainly, when I think of my grandson, I think about the kind of world he will inherit from us. And then I think perhaps Nancy is right and that my grandmother-style is to go on doing things that might make that world just a little better for him—and for all the other babies. They all belong to all of us, don't they? Including the maimed Vietnamese baby.

Getting back to your parole. According to my friends at People's Appeal, parole depends on two things: your conduct inside and your possibilities outside. The first is up to you, but, according to P.A., you have no control over the second and someone must work on getting you an acceptable job and an approved place to live when you get out.

P.A. says there are a number of half-way houses in the Bay Area now, and placing you in one of them should prove no great problem, but that the job is the crucial point, it being so hard to find work now. You've mentioned experience in gardening and carpentry. Is there anything else? Perhaps I should have a complete statement of your training and experience so that I could show it to people.

Love,

Sally

Dear Sally,

I thought i had sent you every document dealing with my case, but i must have left out the report from my probation officer. He is the one who put me here, and you can imagine what he thinks of me. His name is Henry Sanier. I have had no word from him since he recommended putting me away, and i dont expect i ever will again. i will ask my lawyer to contact him and tell him to send you a copy of his report. You will find he judged me a man who worked "sporadically and unwillingly," who drank too much, who kept company with disreputable people, kept irregular hours, no regular address, was hostile and belligerent, who even the army did not want, who was given opportunities (job corps, carpenter apprenticeship program) but "failed to appreciate these opportunities, preferring to drift aimlessly and self-destructively."

i have only one comment to make on his report.

Every word of it is true.

i was a real Mission Bum. Work? We laughed at people who worked. My mother worked. All she got out of it was sore knees and a no-good son who took what he could get from her. Then sometimes i would get sick of cruising around laughing at people who worked. i would wish i could do something. i got into the gardening training or the carpentry apprentice program, excited about learning and doing something. i did learn. My bosses always said i was intelligent and caught on fast. But after a few weeks, something would happen. i would start to feel like i could not breathe. And things would boil up inside of me—i cant explain because i dont understand it myself. Something in me seemed to be asking, "Is this all? Is this all?" And i would fight with my boss, or one day just walk away, as i did from the Job Corps. (There were other good reasons for that, but there is no point in going into them now.)

So that is the man i was. I say *was* because i dont think i am anymore. Something has changed. Did prison change me? Am i rehabilitated? Yes, the change started in here. The change, the overpowering of that Mission Bum, the channeling of all his energy and anger started when i started writing.

The first time I held the pencil, I held it in my fist and drove it straight through the paper (i wasted a lot of paper that way). I crouched on my bunk, hiding, shaking, and wrote my first poem (i didnt know it was a poem) and I felt something happening. Like something struggling to get out of me for years was finally let out. A force, energy that had gone mad, murderous, the longer it was held in. Something there all the time, trying to get free, something I didnt know was in me.

I said I must read for my life, and I know I must write for my life. Now that I am writing I feel that I have the chance of leaving all that chaos and madness behind. When I work in the plate plant or out in the fields my hands move while my brain searches for words to describe those movements, sounds and sights all around me. Sometimes I think that with a real tool in my hand (not standing at a machine) I could fuse the poetry of my mind with the poetry of a tree I am pruning or the wood I am shaping. Then I would not be working in the emptiness that made me explode, that made me shapeless, lost in a void. With my writing to give shape to the world, i dont think i would be lost again.

I have a message for your friend Barbara. Tell her that there are many things I want to do before I die.

1. Be unwatched for one hour
2. Be alone, in silence for one hour
3. Walk down a crowded street, empty street, any street
4. Swim
5. Stand under a shower, alone, for as long as i want
6. Eat a huge bag of cherries and see how far i can spit the pits
7. Fall asleep under a tree, face down in grass
8. Kiss my mother

i dont want to continue the list because i would cover all the paper I bought with the money you sent, and all the paper I could buy in the future. And for years I could go on making that list. After a while I would give up on the list and maybe I would get out of here, and then I would need years, maybe centuries, to do all the things on the list before I die. So I would never have the time to get around to dying.

Peace,

Gary

P.S. About your grandson. No, you wont die from the lack. But he will suffer, whether he knows it or not, from that lack of his fantastic grandmother.

Dear Gary,

Only a minute to write. Barbara's moving out today, Mother arriving tomorrow, and I got stuck for arranging a benefit for the Emergency Food Project.

I took you at your word and showed your letter to Barbara. I don't know how much it had to do with getting her over the worst part, but she did ask questions about you and gave me ten dollars for books or paper or anything else you might need.

That gave me an idea. I wish I could take an order from you for all the books you want; I just can't afford it. But I have friends who can. They're so used to my collecting money that some automatically reach for their wallets when they see me coming. I tapped everyone I saw during the past few days and amassed a small fortune—well, seventy-eight dollars. So send me a list of books you want, in order of preference, and I'll order till I run out of money.

Must run. More soon.

Love,

Sally

Wednesday
May 3

Dear Sally,

Here are a few from a very long list that keeps growing. I had a hard time deciding which ones I wanted most. Youre fabulous!
THE HOUSE OF THE DEAD by Dostoevsky
POVERTY, USA by Abner Hank
MY PRISON STRUGGLE by Joey Banks
DEATH ROW ed. John Susen
COMPLETE PRUNING GUIDE by Robert Kirk
AMERICAN THE RAPED by Gene Marine
DEAR THEO by Van Gogh, ed. Irving Stone
THE PENAL COLONY by Kafka
ELEMENTS OF STYLE by Strunk and White
INCREASING WORD POWER by H.F. Smith

CIVIL DISOBEDIENCE by Thoreau
ANARCHISM by Woodcock
WORKING WITH WOOD by Allen Strong
20th CENTURY POETS ed. Manly Celego
Any of them, not necessarily in that order.

Love,

Gary

Sunday,
May 14

Dear Sally,

By now you have the documents concerning my employment record. i suppose that explains your silence. Being the kind of person you are, you would continue to send me books, etc, just as you would go on with your other causes, even though you decided that getting involved with me was a mistake.

i understand your feelings. i wish to thank you for corresponding with me, and i wish you luck in your many worthwhile activities.

Yours truly,

Gary

Tuesday
May 16

Dear Gary,

Dammit! How could you think I would abandon you now! I would be hurt if I didn't know that having hurt feelings is a luxury you and I haven't time for. I think I understand all the reasons why you're still afraid to count on anyone. But I certainly squirmed when you referred to my "causes." Lost causes, you should say.

But, dear Gary, you're quite wrong if you list yourself among my lost causes. Writing to you, giving you what small help I could, trying to get you parolled (some news on this in a few days, I hope) is the

47

most real, most fulfilling—I have been as grateful to you for letting me help as you have been for my offering the help. And who knows which of us benefits more?

There are many things I do that I don't particularly want to. I would like to drop them and write to you instead. Perhaps I'm being very weak in not doing so, since I don't feel that I accomplish much, while getting one book to you is a more real accomplishment than anything I do all week. Some day maybe I'll be strong enough to sweep many demands out of my life, but in the meantime, you must be patient with me, and if I am silent for a few days (I know, it was two whole weeks) know that it's just impossible for me to write.

Yes, I read your probation officer's evaluation, and, yes, you certainly did rattle around, a perfect nuisance to everyone, including yourself. But that's all over now. That was someone else, not the talented young man who writes such beautiful letters to me.

My mother has been here two weeks now. We run through a standard repertory of scenes that might amuse you:

Scene I

John comes up to the kitchen about noon, where Mother asks how he feels, her assumption being only sick people sleep till noon. John mumbles something, and Mother questions him about his plans for the day, the month, the year, his life. Then she makes a thin, tight line of her mouth and looks at me.

Scene II

Mother sits in the living room listening while teachers and students meet around the dining room table. Much shouting, cussing, laughing. Mother sits with open book, never turning a page. Finally, she says (as I pass through the room as fast as possible, but never fast enough) "Your father always demanded respect from his students."

Scene III

I come home to find Mother has emptied the refrigerator and started defrosting it, just before dinner. There's food all over, melting and dripping, and no room to cook. "Someone had to clean out that mess since you're never at home."

Scene IV

After a phone call, Mother asks, "Who was that?" I try to explain. Usually it has something to do with the November elections. She sets her mouth again. Silence so loud it drowns out my voice. Of course, she's against my candidates. I think she hasn't really been for anyone since Herbert Hoover, who was at least a Stanford man.

Scene V

I take Mother for a ride, thinking she's cooped up too much. "Take me to Durant, where that little tea shop is." I say it isn't there. She insists. We go to Durant and Telegraph. There's a pizza parlour. She looks at the people sprawled on the sidewalk in front, then looks accusingly at me, as if this is my hangout. She asks if I remember the tea shop. I nod and she glares at me, as if I'm responsible for its disappearance.

During the first week I wasn't sure I could stand it. Bob says I should be used to it. Why does it get worse? Bob (both of whose parents are dead) says I'm silly to let it bother me. It was John who labeled and numbered the scenes, and after that I was able to smile inwardly—a little—when one started.

And so I'm learning not to react, especially when I see how helpless she is otherwise. I was shocked to see how much she has failed this past year, how shrunken and dazed she sometimes looks. At eighty what can we expect? Yet, I'd rather see her glowering at us all than nodding in the corner, her fingers twitching.

There. I wasn't going to mention her, but I feel better for having let it all out.

Love,

Sally

P.S. We probably will drive her home to Long Beach next month. I can't imagine she'll be strong enough to make the trip alone. Perhaps we could visit you on the way. I'll start writing to find out what red tape we need to untangle to accomplish that. P.P.S. I ordered all the books. They should start arriving in another week or so.

Saturday
May 20

Dear Sally,

You didnt tell me whether your mother had seen you writing to me. Ready for Scene VI?

Scene VI

Mother asks what youre writing. You tell her. Then she says, "You mean you are writing to a criminal, even trying to get him out, to turn him loose on society again?" She goes to her room and locks the door so no mad criminals can get at her.

Poor Sally. Between your mother nagging at you and me nagging at you, you probably would like to tell us both where to go. I apologize. You know, its this place. A kind of fear comes over me sometimes, and I read all your letters over and tell myself that someone cares about me, but theres always the fear that something will change your mind and—but I promise I wont think that again. If you dont write, its because you cant.

I am starting to write a novel. It will tell about a mean, rebellious boy growing up in the Mission District of San Francisco. Im going to call it BATTLES because it is, chapter by chapter, one battle after another, in school, at home, on the street. It is very hard to write. I had it all planned out. But then, when I started writing, I remembered more things and tried to put them in. Now the plan is all mixed up, and I cant keep track of anything. This is a different kind of writing, not like poetry. It makes me more tired, but not uplifted the way writing poetry makes me feel. But a novel would be easier to sell than poetry. Some writers are making millions writing down all the things i used to try to forget.

Ive already filled out Request for Visitor forms for you. Therell be more of them for you to fill out when you come. The thought of really seeing you is like an electric charge that I can plug into any time I feel low.

My lawyer from P.A. was here with more papers to sign, and he said something about jobs. What jobs? More surprises? Youre holding out on me.

Love,

Gary

Saturday
May 27

Dear Gary,

I didn't want to tell you till I was sure. If you get out some time this year, Sam will be able to use you at least one day a week. He says you must be prepared to hammer nails or haul trash or whatever is needed on small jobs like the ones he does, and he will pay you the equivalent of apprentice carpenter wages.

Barbara has moved back into her house (which she had rented to a family while she tried commune living). She has a big garden that's overgrown and needs to be put in shape. She could use you a couple of times a month (depending on how much money she has; her working hours vary). Another couple, Jake and Judy Meyer (they're our oldest married friends, did I mention them before?) also could use some yard work two or three times a month.

I wish I could offer you some work here. Certainly there are enough things falling apart and the yard is a constant struggle, but our income seems just to keep up with our commitments. (The heaviest drain right now is some regular help to the Farm Workers organizers.)

Your lawyer feels that these jobs would be enough. Since all your work will be in Berkeley, you might look into the possibility of a half-way house on this side of The Bay. I'm sure your lawyer will take this up with you next.

Love,

Sally

Thursday
June 1

Dear Sally,

What kind of magic do you send? A letter from you must be charged with super energy. I read one and I feel like I could float up, right through the ceiling into the sky. If my writing has slowed down, I suddenly have new inspiration. Its life you send in. You are life, entering this House of the Dead.

Yes, the Dostoevsky book arrived first and I finished it this morning. A strange book, about a strange prison. In some ways more brutal. The flogging must have killed many prisoners, if they did not die of the cold or the bad food in Siberia. And yet it was more humane than what I see. Families were allowed to live nearby. Even strangers came to the fence to give food and clothing on Christmas.

51

So the ordinary people of Russia did not hate and fear the prisoners but saw all prisoners as unfortunates. I cried when I read that because I know our people dont feel that way and even after I get out Ill always be treated like Im not quite human.

I hope i am wrong about that. A few men have left prison to become famous leaders of political groups. But you know how I feel about political groups, so that way is not open to me. I am just a "common" criminal. When I get out, if I can survive long enough to write the truth about my life, maybe I will be able to show people that all prisoners are political prisoners and that, the way things are now, every sentence is a life sentence.

I dont want to go to a half-way house. From what I have heard, such places are run almost like a prison with as many rules and regulations and stupid threats and penalties for not obeying. And i get chills when i think of living with ex-convicts. I want to get as far away as possible from anything that will remind me of life here. There is no such thing as half-way to freedom. In a house like that a man is not free, not a man.

Half-way houses show the contradiction in the authorities attitudes. The main rule for a parollee is that he must not associate with ex-convicts. Yet in a half-way house he lives, eats and sleeps with them. What makes it all right? Power. If the authorities can exercise power, forcing ex-convicts to live together, make rules, control, dominate, then what was forbidden suddenly becomes better than just leaving a man to live alone. This is illogical but typical of the system.

Which is what i want to forget. I want to be left alone to find myself. Is that so much to ask? All I want is a quiet room away from men who have been conditioned by life in cages. But if theres no other way, then it will have to be a half-way house. I dont know why im saying all this when it will be months before i can even get a hearing. But just to go on day by day I have to act like parole is certain.

Am I really going to see you in a few days?

No, you didnt tell me about the Meyers. Tell me all about these great people. I know theyre great because theyre your friends.

Love,

Gary

Dear Gary,

My mother is staying on much longer than we expected, perhaps permanently. She has become quite feeble since last year's visit, but was too proud to tell us that she cannot manage alone anymore. One of her neighbors in Long Beach called and confirmed my suspicions that she had not been getting along as well as she led us to believe.

Bob's immediate reaction was typical of him. He threw his arms around her and said, "Well, of course, you're going to stay right here and help us make a real family!" And promptly left with Millie (a substitute teacher at his school) to attend a meeting, saying cheerful things about the extended family. Whereas, in the back of my mind I am thinking, "The extended family is a good idea, but couldn't I take in someone else's mother?" I could put an ad in the paper:

> Dignified Granny, prefers short-haired dogs and children, clean, well-read, conservative

> will trade for

> Old suffragette who doesn't mind mess and noise, drinks a bit and when tipsy sings old Wobbly songs (tennis shoes optional).

What I'm really sorry about is that, since we won't be driving her back, we won't be able to visit you after all. It would have been so good to see you face to face.

I understand your feeling about half-way houses. I haven't come up with any bright ideas yet, but I'll keep working on the housing question. Rents are so high!

I thought I had told you about Jake and Judy Meyer. They came here in the early fifties from New York. They were the first New Yorkers I met, and I can still remember how the air seemed to crackle around them, how ideas and knowledge spurted out of them with an intensity I had never seen. (Twenty-odd years here have slowed them down a bit.)

The very first thing that happened to the Meyers when they came here was that both lost the jobs they came here to take. (Both were highly qualified teachers with a string of degrees, experience and publication.) That was during the time of Joseph McCarthy, when many good people lost jobs because of a club they joined in college or a petition they signed. I met Judy at nursery school where both of us had our children and she broke down and cried (Judy's very emotional and cries a lot even today) telling me that they were broke, couldn't find work, and people in their profession were afraid even to speak to them. She said she was frightened because Jake had withdrawn into himself and sat at home reading about old *pogroms* (they are Jews) and had not spoken for days.

I brought them home to dinner that night. Jake came out of his silence into brilliant talk. We hit it off right away and had a lovely time (except that they quarreled after dinner, but they always do, and some day we're going to get used to it).

We were able to get Judy a job selling real estate. That gave Jake a chance to brush up on some business skills and he soon got into tax accounting. Both of them started in these fields at the right time, and with their ability made piles of money, much more than they ever could have in teaching. Sometimes they talk about going back to teaching now that the wind has shifted, but I don't suppose they ever will. "I've lost my idealism," says Jake. "You mean your nerve," snaps Judy, and they're off again.

If they sound bitter, they have good reason, for, on top of everything else, they have suffered real tragedy. A daughter died of drug overdose three years ago. Their son went to Canada to escape the draft and settled there. The other daughter is studying in Europe. They live and wait for letters.

Jake never makes promises, but he offered the gardening work for you and hinted that he might be able to do more. He is an invaluable contact.

You'll laugh when you see them together. Judy is tiny, not even five feet tall, very emotional (she cries when I mention your letters, let alone read them to her!) talks a lot, always hugs people and mothers them. Jake is tall and heavy with a deep, slow voice, like a big bear. He speaks coolly, analytically, and eyes Judy coldly when she bubbles over. Often it's a cool thrust from him, in the midst of her overflow, that starts a quarrel. At first I believed they were on the verge of divorce all the time, but I've almost begun to see their quarrels as a ritual. Oh, they've become alike in one way—both now have quite white hair, Jake's thicker and bushier and (this year) longer than Judy's.

Mother's calling—must run.

Love,

Sally

P.S. More bad news. The reason you haven't received your Free Weekly is that it no longer exists. Finished. Folded. It was inevitable. Surprising that it held out this long. Yet the end came as a shock, maybe because we got used to it hovering on the brink, yet always surviving for another issue. The saddest part of it (to me personally) is that Yves is going to an educational center in Mexico for a while, and Mary has taken a job on a women's movement magazine in New York. Two more good people gone, at least for a while. As I get older, friends become more precious and losing contact with them, more painful.

Friday
June 30

Dear Sally,

Ive been spending most of the last couple of weeks working hard on my novel (instead of bouncing a letter right back to you the minute I hear from you) but now I have hit a block. But I know I can use Sally-magic to get through it. Writing to you will loosen up everything.

Having your mother with you, along with your son, will make your life more difficult. Your house must seem like a half-way house without rules—your mother in transition, going to the end of life, and your son in transition too. Well, I guess were all in transition. You are really a great person. You say your husband acts on what he believes in, but you do too. Other women would have found some excuse for putting their old mother away somewhere, one of those places where they wait to die. Death Row, the same as in any prison. I am afraid to think where my mother will end up if I am not able to take care of her.

I am afraid when I think of other things too. Now that there is a real chance of getting out of here soon I cant stop thinking, dreaming of freedom. And I am afraid. The old cons say that every sentence is a life sentence. They mean that when I get out of here, the police will grab me any time a liquor store is robbed, or a gas station, or anything. I will be an automatic suspect when they dont have any real ones and need to improve their arrest and conviction record. They can easily push a witness to identify anyone they bring in. Then comes the pressure to cop a plea for a short term, and the whole process goes round and round again. Dont say I exaggerate. Ive met too many men here who never escaped that cycle—like getting stuck in a revolving door, one of them said.

Jake and Judy sound like interesting people. The way they fight reminds me of my friends, Joe and Margie. They had to get married when they were sixteen, but that was all right because they love each other and they love children. Still, they fight all the time except when they are dreaming up crazy schemes to make a million. They live on dreams, and each time one dream starts to wear out they have a terrible fight. Then they make up, and Margie gets pregnant. If theyre still together, they have been married six years now and probably have six children. They had three when I knew them, but one died when it was only a few months old, so they have that in common with your friends too.

Of course, they are not really like your friends. They are losers like all the people I know. Their dreams will never come true.

Maybe most dreams dont come true. I used to think that people who were not poor had everything their own way. But all your friends had dreams that did not come true. Even Dennis. He wrote me a note about my last batch of poems. ''Whatever youre producing, youre writing, and that makes you more alive than anyone who isnt.'' You said he had stopped writing.

Now tell me about Millie.

Love,

Gary

56

Dear Gary,

Has your lawyer talked to you about the letters he got? He seemed to think they would be very helpful, but he doesn't expect you'll get a hearing before fall, September or October.

This is just hello and good-bye. There's a funding crisis at the Free Clinic and I've been up late at meetings all week. Work also piling up at campaign headquarters so forgive me if letters get skimpy. I'll write more when possible.

Sally

Sunday
July 16

Dear Sally,

Just got copies of letters my lawyer got from the witnesses of the robbery. Of course, they all say they never saw me. He has statements from Sol and Angie too, saying I didnt know anything about the robbery but I dont know how much the word of two convicts matter.

My lawyer says the letters could help some or not at all, since technically I am not here for that crime but for violation of probation. Mainly the parole board will be interested in what chance I have for keeping out of trouble in the future.

My carrots are up, but my tomato plant looks sick. I think the soil is too acid. I am trying to get them to let me start a compost heap with kitchen scraps. That is more complicated than making parole!

Love,

Gary

Sunday
July 23

Dear Gary,

I keep trying to see that Adult Authority man about you but simply can't get to him. I wrote him a letter telling him about our correspondence and the high hopes I have for you if you are released, but your lawyer said my "high hopes" don't count as expert opinion on your (excuse the expression) rehabilitation. He said giving positive assurance of continuing interest after your release would help more, so I added something about the jobs you'll have.

Must run. Someone just called to say they can't find the precinct lists. I don't know why, whenever something goes wrong they call me. And I vowed I wouldn't get so involved in this election.

Love,

Sally

Tuesday
July 25

Dear Sally,

Im trying to resign myself to not hearing much from you until the election is over. I promise I wont panic. I wont even say youre wasting your time. I will remind myself that youre doing your best to try to make this world better. And I will remind myself that my friend Sally would not have become my friend if she was not the kind of person who must answer every call for help.

Dennis has written several times about my poems. In his last letter he told me something I didnt know, something that started so many thoughts spinning in my head that I couldnt sleep for the past two nights. He said I dont need a high school diploma to go to a junior college. Anyone over eighteen can go. Now I remember you said your son John had not finished high school but was thinking about going to junior college. Dennis says the college is free and there is even a fund to help students buy books. He said I would only have to give an address in the college district. Maybe I could use your address? Would that be dishonest?

What I am trying to say, what I am afraid to say, is what I have been thinking and dreaming of ever since I read his letter. That I could go to college and begin to really educate myself.

The problem would be supporting myself and going to school at the same time. One possible solution. If, in addition to the part-time jobs working for your friends, you could find someone who would give me room and board in exchange for handy-man work? No, thats much harder than your other miracles. It is one thing to ask people to give work to an ex-convict. But who would let an ex-convict live in their house?

It is a hopeless dream. But thinking about it helps me to get through the days, just the way your election helps you.

Love,

Gary

P.S. Dennis offered to read the first few chapters of my novel. I know he is only doing this out of friendship for you, and I probably shouldnt bother him with all my junk.

Thursday
August 3

Dear Gary,

It's not that I didn't think of it before, but that I felt my mother's moving in permanently would make it impossible. I can't ask Bob to give up his study, and there's no telling how long John will be here. That means all the bedrooms are occupied. When Mother moved in, my deep, unspoken concern was that I no longer had a room to offer you.

Then—while reading your letter I was sitting down here in The Dungeon (an unfortunate name considering the offer I'm about to make). It's a tiny room with a concrete floor (it used to be a wash-room) but I have some rush mats I could cover the floor with, and there's heat and a big window looking out over one of the nicest slopes of our garden. I wish I could offer you more, and I wish you could see it before making a decision.

Bob agrees with me that we need more bookshelves built and help with gardening and painting we've gotten behind on. You could set your own hours for working off whatever you think board and room would be worth. (That shouldn't be much for a vegetarian in The Dungeon).

You mustn't think that Dennis is just doing me a favor by reading your work. I had a long talk with him yesterday. He is genuinely interested in you and says he has gathered together a stack of catalogues, admission forms and other information on the college, which he will send to you so that your dreams may become concrete plans.

Dennis and I became friends when I was still writing, more than ten years ago, and signed up for his creative writing class. He had already stopped writing, saying that everyone wants to write but few will admit that they might do more creative work in the long run by helping others with more talent. A few days in his class is enough to convince anyone (at least for a while) that nothing is more important than writing. Besides teaching at the college he gives hours and hours to special arts programs, especially in poor areas, and he's wonderful there too. His being black helps. Deep tan, really, with wavy, silky hair and a deep, rich voice, with an occasional broad *a* left over from his New England childhood. Dennis lives in a little house not far from us, which he sometimes shares with other bachelors. He looks very young, not much older than you, but he must be close to forty, since he's been teaching at least 15 years. I think it must be his enthusiasm for beauty, for any effort at creative work, that keeps him so young. His Bible is Rilke's LETTERS TO A YOUNG POET. He told me he had already written to the publisher and ordered a copy to be sent to you.

It's awfully late and quite pitch-black out. The Dungeon window looks directly into a wooded slope, no sight of moon or light from street lamps. Sometimes, when I sit down here, I can imagine myself away from the city entirely, in a peaceful still place where night is really dark and quiet and restful.

Yossarian keeps getting up and going to the door, to see if I'm ready to go up to bed yet. But, although I need the sleep, I keep wanting to wait until the rest of the house is quiet and everyone is sleeping. I've been down here since dinner, speaking to no one, like a little fox hiding and licking her wounds.

Wounds? What a silly thing to write. I'm just tired and, as usual when I'm tired, wondering what it's all about and whether I'm accomplishing anything at all. The only place where I feel no doubts is here, in these letters between you and me, in our victory (for we will win!) in getting you out of there.

Love,

Sally

Dear Sally,

I read your letter six times to make sure. You really are offering me a room in your house! You say it like we had been talking about it for weeks. This is your way of doing things for people. Like you are doing nothing. I almost couldnt believe it, and at the same time I was not surprised at all.

Yes, my dear, wonderful Sally, I accept your offer of room and board. In exchange for which, I will devote fifteen hours per week to your house and garden. I once made a tall pine bookcase, finishing it with a clear plastic coating, then sanding and finishing again, three or four times. It looked much better than the usual stain and varnish job. Im sure I could do a nice one for you if you like the look of natural wood? Then I could gradually work my way up and down your hillside garden. The fall (I feel sure now of getting out of here this fall) is the best time for getting everything cleaned up. Your hillside probably needs careful pruning. Erosion is a problem if too much is taken off. Especially in a slide area. And painting has always been one of my favorite kinds of work. I once worked for a man who showed me how to paint properly. The important thing is not the brush work but the preparation, cleaning the walls, masking the windows and trim.

The Dungeon will be fine. You would not apologize for it if you had seen some of the places I have lived in. You say it has heat and a window looking out on the garden. It sounds like paradise. A quiet place, removed from the rest of the house. A perfect room for a writer. When I am not in school or working, I will be able to climb down to this quiet room to be alone with my thoughts and inspirations.

I am worried about one thing. I know you want me. I know your heart very well now. I would not refuse an offer from it. No more than I would refuse the speaking of my own heart. You and I, we know each other now. But what about the others? Bob, John, your mother, your friends? They give money for books for a convict, even hire him to work for them. But do they want him to sit in the same

room with them? Live with them? I dont want to make trouble for
you.

Love,

Gary

Dear Gary,

I've given up trying to see Agtente of the Adult Authority. I bom-
barded him with letters, outlining your case and asking for an appointment, but all I got back are forms to fill out and suggestions that
I put whatever I want to say him in writing. I'm working on a statement now.

About the people in our house. There's no point in pretending
Mother is happy about it, but I agonized over her for a long time
before I decided that her values must not overwhelm mine. As soon as
I thought of it that way, I almost laughed, thinking that I'm only
adding you to a situation she already sees as beyond all reason. I hope
you will be able to overlook anything in her manner that seems insult-
ing. She is so frail now—when you see her you'll be able to forgive
her silly attitudes.

John is indifferent. He may not even notice you. He's absorbed in
his plans to try college. Since you'll both be at Bay College, you may
end up having something in common.

Bob is more positive, though in a rather condescending way
(toward me, not you). Said something about it being good for me,
that I looked more optimistic about you than about anything else. He
was too busy to say more; he and Millie were off to another meeting.
A split has developed in the teachers' union and Bob is leading the
forces on one side. I'm not sure what the issues are. I've lost interest,
and it's not surprising that Bob finds others to work with him.

There was a time when I was more involved than Bob himself. I
nagged him until he joined the union, while he resisted because he
was afraid membership would hurt his chances for advancement.

Then the union became respectable and I lost interest. Not that there's anything wrong with being respectable. But when I poured coffee and listened to meetings here, I heard a lot of talk about nothing that concerned the real issues. Bob's group is absorbed in strategy to get control of the union, while parents I talk to are afraid to send their children to school for fear of the violence no one will admit exists. Bob shrugs when I talk about violence and says it is exaggerated, but he's always selling his principal on projects he can do outside of actual teaching. Sometimes I think he hasn't changed at all since I first met him and he talked about "getting to the top." Pushing him onto a different field of action didn't change his basic nature, so it's no wonder his deafness is more pronounced when I disagree with him, no wonder he would turn to people who admire him just the way he is.

I'm becoming querulous. My eyes burn and my neck aches, and one shouldn't write anything in the middle of the night even if there's no other time.

Love,

Sally

Saturday
August 26

Dear Sally,

Great news! Peoples Appeal presented my case—stressing revocation of probation for a misdemeanor. It looks very, very good, almost sure. The lawyer just left me. He said, "I think we will have you out of here for Thanksgiving."

I go before the parole board on October 6. Lawyer said, "I can't see what could go wrong, especially with you set up to live with the Morgans."

Gary

Sept. 7

Dear Gary,

I finally got a letter from Agtente that sounded aware of our existence. Here's a copy of the letter I've written him. If you can think of *anything* else I can do before you go before the board, let me know fast.

Love,

Sally

10 Crown Court
Berkeley, Calif.
September 8, 19—

G. Q. Agtente
California Adult Authority
Sacramento, California

RE: Wilson, Gary G-49930

Dear Mr. Agtente:

Thank you for your letter of September 1. Since Gary Wilson's parole hearing is scheduled, I believe, for October 6, it seems more appropriate to try to convey what I believe is relevant to his case by means of a letter rather than wait for the chance of an interview. I am sending a copy of this letter to the Southern California Correctional Farm for Mr. Wilson's permanent addenda, and a copy also to State Assemblyman Burton's office.

It has been almost a year since I first became interested in this young man through a letters-to-prisoners program. Before I had found out anything about the reasons for his imprisonment or his background, I was struck by the originality of his writing and the wide-ranging interests he displayed in his letters. Later, I was even more impressed by his avid reading and sent him books on a wide range of subjects. But most impressive has been his determined use and development of his talent for writing poetry, his determination to turn every feeling and experience into a creative expression. When he expressed the hope that he might someday go to college, I was determined to do all I could to further that goal.

I believe that if Wilson had enjoyed different family circumstances —if he had not been raised solely by an overworked mother, if he had lived elsewhere than a "housing project," his life might have been different. Wilson is in prison as a secondary result of a charge to which he was induced to plead guilty (a robbery all witnesses of which have declared they never saw him) and there seems to be a real question of whether due process was observed in the courts. The violation which led to his imprisonment was a simple drunk and disorderly charge, an instance of usual behavior among young men, certainly never leading to imprisonment. In his case it constituted a violation of probation and resulted in this extreme penalty.

Because he is an extremely alert, sensitive, intelligent person, it would seem he has a better chance of being a productive member of society if he is released as promptly as possible so that his education can go forward. He has been accepted at Bay Junior College where an instructor has taken a strong interest in his case. A Berkeley contractor has offered him part-time carpentry work, and two other families guarantee him gardening work (see enclosed statements). I have offered a place to stay to guarantee satisfactory living conditions as long as he needs them.

The fact that Wilson dropped out of high school does not surprise me nor should it be considered a mark against his chances for success in college. My own son became disgusted with high school and is now performing successfully as a college student. Wilson shows marked interest in literature and writing and has already published one of his poems.

What seems to me absolutely critical is that he be given a chance to build on this foundation of self-education and enthusiasm for higher learning while he still possesses it. I am fearful that a longer confinement would deaden his hopes and his resolve. It would seem that successful rehabilitation would be best served by letting him go out

65

into the community to pursue his real interests and make a constructive life for himself now that he has the chance to do so.

I hope you will give these circumstances your closest attention when his case comes before you for review.

Very truly yours,

Sarah Morgan
(Mrs. Robert Morgan)

Copies to:
Southern California Correctional Farm
Assemblyman John Burton
Members of California Adult Authority

Wednesday
September 20

Dear Sally,

Frozen panic since reading your last letter. Tension almost unbearable. Fear that something might go wrong. All seems sure, perfect. After so many years wasted life, everything has changed and is streaming forward, like a great wave. I wake up at night shaking. Terrified something might go wrong.

Days are weird. Even more frightening. Tense, edgy, I feel I am being watched for behavior that would contradict your letter, would erase everything I have done. I imagine crazy things. It is all I can do to stay cool, to take one day at a time, not to suddenly spill out feelings that would make trouble. My senses are so tight that other people are unbearable. I keep to myself, withdraw into myself. Search for a quiet, safe place to wait.

Each night I mark off one more day on the calendar. I try to write out the tension. I write and write. Sorry, need more paper.

No, theres nothing more you can do. Nothing to do but wait.

Love,

Gary

Dear Sally,

I used to take out favorite letters of yours to read when I was feeling low. Some of your letters I know almost by heart.

Last night I read through all of them, and the carbons of mine. Like an outsider reading the correspondence of two strangers. I cant describe the feeling it gave me. The feeling of watching someone listening and caring and coming closer to someone in need, and that someone in need (me) becoming healed and whole and real and strong and able to reach out in friendship, like a man. And then two equals, friends. And then, more. Something like lovers. No, not lovers, that is the easy way to try to say how close we have come. The only way I can say it is this: have you noticed how our letters, the last month or so, resemble each other? Partly that's because I have learned so much from you, and I guess I imitate you. But it is more than that. It is like we both speak with one voice. Because our two souls have met and have joined.

The fall quarter at Bay College begins today, according to the schedule Dennis sent me. I had hoped to be out in time for this quarter, but I guess I will be too late. I will have to sign up for the winter quarter. To pass the time, I have been making schedules for myself.

I want to try to carry a full schedule of classes on Monday, Wednesday and Friday, four classes of 3 units each. I have marked the ones I most want to take: Creative Writing, Shakespeare, Political Science, Psychology.

On Tuesdays I will work for Sam Jones, then for Barbara or Jake and Judy Meyer on alternate Thursdays. Ill take care of your garden and other projects on weekends. Im already working on a sketch of the bookcase. I need the dimensions of the wall you want it on. (Making a sketch may seem premature, but I guess you understand that I must fill time with plans.)

In the evenings I can go down to the dungeon to study. That leaves only the very early morning hours for writing. But I am used to waking up before five here (vegetarians dont need much sleep) and I should be able to get in two or three hours of writing before anyone else is out of bed. Except you and Yossarian. On weekends I might take a holiday from writing and go with you two on your early morning walk. God, I just thought of it—saw it—getting up and just walking out. Walking down the street. Anywhere I want to go.

I want to try to spend Sunday afternoons with my mother. Aside from that, I have no desire to go to San Francisco, not for a while. It would remind me of too many painful things. I want a clean fresh start.

Love,

Gary

10/1

Dear Gary,

The wall is 15 × 9. It really should be covered entirely with bookshelves. I think we could fill the whole wall with just what has spilled over onto tables, odd corners, stair landings. Most of our books are paperback but there are quite a few odd-sized hardbounds, so spacing of shelves could be irregular.

Your schedule sounds like enough for three men. I'm afraid you'll be so eager to do everything you'll wear yourself out. You should plan to take it easy for a few days, just to ease your transition. But, there now, I won't tell you what to do. You've had enough of people telling you what to do.

Dennis says a few classes are open throughout the quarter but probably not the ones you want. He said you are certainly welcome in his class whenever you get out, though you might not be able to get officially enrolled for credit till next quarter. But he's probably told you that already.

Only a few more days till your hearing. I won't wish you luck. I'm sure everything will go all right. I can't imagine—I won't imagine that anything could go wrong.

Love,

Sally

Friday
October 6

Dear Sally,

It was all over in five minutes. Two men sitting with my file in front of them. They pulled out a couple of papers. I couldnt see which ones. Asked a couple of questions, the usual, rehabilitation and attitude. I gave them the usual answers. And that was all. I keep going over and over what they said and how they looked at me, trying to figure out what they were thinking, will they recommend for me—I could drive myself crazy this way!

MONDAY

It's over. I've got a date. December 1. That means I have to be out of here by then. My lawyer says he will try to get me out before. They often let you go sooner, once its official. Ive packed my stuff and sent it for inspection. That way if they suddenly walk in and say, "Time to Go," and escort me to the bus station (that's what they do, they want to make sure you get as far away from here as possible) Ill be ready. Ill telephone you as soon as I know for sure when Ill get there.

I think Im getting out of here just in time.

I dont care what I say now. I have my date, and they cant keep me for anything I say.

The tension is so bad that anyone here could be in danger of his life for a cigarette or a wrong word.

They were measuring my cell yesterday, to build in another bunk, to stuff two men into this tiny cage.

I wont write to you again. Ten days or forty days. Each day when I wake up I will say, maybe today is the day. I can hang on now, in silence, like a monk meditating. Waiting until I see you and hear your voice and take your hand.

Soon,

Gary

69

FREEDOM

"GOD, what a lousy showing!" Barbara holds her cup out to me and I fill it. It is the third time she has said it. No one answers. No one listens. She uncrosses and recrosses her legs, then swings them to the side and tucks them up on the sofa. The slit in her skirt opens high on her thigh. Mother looks at her thigh and frowns. "Lousy showing!" No one responds. "Thanks, Sally."

The others mention the small victories.

"The farm workers made it, close, but they made it."

"The conservation bill was a sure thing from the start. Who would have thought everyone would come together on that?"

I pour dark brown consolation into cups held out. But these two don't need consolation. They shake their heads in unison at me and smile through me, at one another. Bob looks slightly puffed, his bald head shiny like a taut balloon. Millie breathes deeply, as though she is blowing up his balloon-head. Is it still a flirtation or has it become an affair? Where do you do it? At your apartment, Millie? In some little closet behind a classroom? Or have you brought her to our own bed when I am not home?

I look into Millie's eyes, and I try to hate her, but I can't. She is thinner since her divorce. Her lips quiver slightly as she smiles at me. Her narrow, oriental eyes go as wide as they can as if she is asking me for something, just a small loan. Just the loan of my husband till she gets through all this? Someone to hold her steady for a bit, to stop the quiver of her lips from spreading throughout her body, stop her body from quivering and wriggling like Barbara's?

It would be easier to hate Bob. His neck stiffens, and his eyes go bleak and hard with shame when he looks at me. But his jaw is set. He has clamped his teeth down, hard and defiant, on some nourishment he wants, something I can't give him, and he won't let go. Wide-eyed, uncritical admiration from a lonely woman twenty years younger than I. Whipped cream. I've never given him that, even twenty years ago. It's what he wants but not what he needs. Who am I to say? Still, it makes him puffy and bloated.

"More coffee, Sam?"

"Yes, thank you." His voice is so clean and crisp, like clear water. "We were looking at your little book of Chinese poetry." He and Dennis, leaning against the bookcase, glancing from time to time at the flickering television set, but already distant from the results and analysis of results being repeated over and over. Their voices mingle, clear water over smooth rock.

"Dennis?" He shakes his head and frowns at the line his finger touches. Dark finger on the white page, darker against the white. Dark-skinned people should always be illuminated by brightness, set off against white. Dennis cares nothing for politics; I would be surprised if he even voted.

But Sam, poor Sam voted. "For the first time you're a voter, enfranchised finally at . . ."

"Fifty-three."

"How does it feel?"

Sam smiles. His smile is open and clear, but it makes hard, sad lines all around his jaw. "While I was marking the ballot, I felt very ceremonious and even triumphant. But now . . ." He nods to the television screen. ". . . I wonder if I didn't jinx the whole thing."

". . . lousy showing," Barbara adds from across the room.

Dennis's insistent finger taps the page, and he and Sam bend their heads over it again.

John and his new girlfriend lie on the floor in front of the fire. No one else can get near the fire. No one looks at them. They are aggressively supine, the girl's long hair draped across John's chest. A languid, sexual pose, coldly presented to embarrass us older, more inhibited folk. I'd like to walk over them, one, two, left foot on her hip, right foot on his belly, and stand in front of the fire and see if I could surprise them into a human reaction, a look, an act that would connect with one of us. No, it wouldn't work. They lie in outer space, safely confined in my living room.

"Coffee?" They move slowly, silently, hold out their cups, drop their heads back onto the rug. The girl chirps, "Thank you," like a ten-year-old at a birthday party. She has been married twice and has a child.

Judy sits down cross-legged beside them and begins to talk, bobbing her white head. Judy will accept the role they assign her, if only she can be close to them, giving love, as we all need to give love. John and the girl nod languidly at Judy and she talks faster and faster. I can't hear what she says. She holds her cup up and out to me, but her head bends down to them.

I look across her in time to see Jake turn his glance away from her, turn his back on the whole room and look through the window, intently, a distant gaze all the way across the bay to San Francisco. They have been quarreling again. That's why Judy talks so much and Jake is silent except to turn wilting glances on her.

"More coffee, Jake?"

"Thank you." He makes a sarcastic but resigned smile.

"How do you account for it?"

Jake purses his lips and squints toward the far distance, beyond The City, beyond to the invisible ocean. Jake will give us an analysis of the extent of our losses this time, something cool and exact, something we all should have seen, could have calculated. But not yet. He is not ready. His audience is not ready. Nor his orchestra. Yes. The instruments of his orchestra are just starting the jarring tune-up, warm-up noises. Only when they are ready will the conductor come on stage.

So I have traveled my little circle again, and ended up back where I began, where Mother sits stiffly on the sofa with squirming, suffering Barbara, who repeats the same, unanswerable lament over and over. "...lousy...lousy showing..." Mother keeps her stiff separation from the very air Barbara disturbs as she moves. I can read your thoughts, Mother. I can look straight through your eyes at us all. Angry, victorious eyes. Why?

Your eyes march around the room. Across the dimply thighs Barbara exposes as she crosses, uncrosses, folds her legs. Divorcee, tramp. Two heads, light and dark, bent over a book. One a traitor to his country, the other, worse. Not because he's black, "..a homosexual, a pervert, isn't he?" Yes, Mother, no Mother. Your eyes soften on Millie, modestly dressed, polite, quiet. Orientals have strong families, raise daughters strictly, that's what you should have done, break that head-strong spirit before your daughter.... But Mother, Millie too is divorced, and she is after my husband. Already the eyes have hardened again, this time on Bob. The old, sad look, more of disappointment than dislike. Disappointment that Bob is Bob and not Father. Too many rough edges. Your daughter's mistake, one of your daughter's many mistakes.

Now something like horror, something hurt glistens in your eyes, and I know you are looking at John. Had you hoped that something of Father would come through in the next generation? You cannot look for long at John. Your eyes flicker over Judy and on to Jake, your glance now hard again and totally unforgiving. Negroes you tolerate, but Jews, never. Their energy, their quickness, the very pace of their thought violated Berkeley, your Berkeley, your university, your life. A wind from the east swept across your warm California, your quiet backyard, chilled it, woke it, and you hated the fresh wind and you called it, Jews.

You do not even look at me as I bend to pour your coffee. You looked at all the others. Now look at me. Look at me as you used to. Mother, I have fallen and hurt my knee, my head, my heart. Mother, kiss it and make it well. No. All that is gone, swept away, and you sit in the midst of your enemies. Look, everyone. You ask why we lost again. Here is the answer. She voted, not for anything, but against us. Ask her. Never mind. She won't answer.

A growl. In the corner, Yossarian is suddenly awake, springing up as I look toward him, looking at me, rushing to me. A bark ending in another growl. "What is it?" He runs to the front door, stands stiff and growling. "Stop that, Yossarian." He usually barks when someone comes, but not this growling. The doorbell rings, and I go to answer it. Yossarian is wild, his barking loud enough to drown out everyone. They all watch as I open the door. I keep my fingers in Yossarian's collar. He has never bitten anyone. "Quiet!" I open the door.

A tall man, thin, long face, blonde hair to his collar. He wears tan pants and shirt and a dark windbreaker jacket. The sleeves are too short. Long arms, long, thin body. Long, thin face. Eyes narrow, lips thin and pale. Sad mouth, turned down. Familiar. Whose mouth does it remind me of? Oh, yes, Mother's mouth.

"Sally." He clutches a big envelope, holds it to his chest. A friend of John's? student of Bob's? No. A suitcase on one side of him, a box on the other. He bends to pick up the suitcase, and I catch a strong whiff of alcohol. Our faces are almost on a level as he rises again; then he is above, to his full height, his thin mouth twisting at one corner into a crooked smile.

Even when I know, I hesitate. "Gary!" He is different from what I expected. How different? Tall, pale, just as he said. How different? "Well, Gary, for heaven's sake! Come in! Don't mind Yossarian. Stop it, Yossarian."

76

He holds out the envelope to me, swings the suitcase forward, and steps over the threshold. He stumbles. His long body falls forward like a tree, stiff and tall. Envelope thrown to the right, suitcase to the left, he crashes down and lies there. Yossarian has two paws on his back, his bared fangs at Gary's neck. No sound. No movement.

Bob pulls Yossarian off, banishes him to his corner, helps Gary to his feet. "Are you all right?" I see by Bob's look that he smells the liquor too.

"Bob, this is Gary Wilson."

A moment of puzzlement, then recognition. Bob grabs his hand and shakes it. "When did you get out? Why didn't you call? How'd you find your way here?"

"They let me out this morning. Put me on the bus. That's how they do things. No warning, nothing." His voice is thick and slow. "On the bus all day. Then, when I got to Oakland, figured, so close, I'd surprise you. Hitched a ride all the way to Spruce Street."

Bob lets go of his hand, and Gary sways. Who would give him a ride in that condition? He keeps squinting. So drunk he can't see. I laugh and he looks at me. He doesn't know whether to laugh with me. So, you've been celebrating. Of course, why not?

He frowns as if remembering something. He looks down at the floor, then bends and picks up the envelope. He hands it to me, Carefully printed across it:

THE CORRESPONDENCE BETWEEN
SALLY MORGAN AND GARY WILSON
PRESERVED FOR PRESENTATION TO HER
ON THE DAY HIS FREEDOM IS WON

He looks at me, then squints, frowns and draws back stiffly. He has seen beyond me, seen the living room full of people, silent, watching him. His surprise has gone all wrong. The presentation of our letters, our moment of triumph falls as flat as he did. Never mind. It doesn't matter.

I take his hand. It is clammy and limp. I wave the envelope in my other hand. "Everyone, this is Gary. He's free." I turn back to Gary. "We've been holding a wake here, for all our dead election hopes. You're almost the first good news we've had all night. Come in and meet everyone."

I put the envelope on the bookshelf. Bob drags in the box from the porch, shuts the door, and puts Gary's suitcase and box beside it.

I take Gary around the room, as I had taken the coffee pot around. His body is taut when it brushes against mine, his hand limp in mine. I identify each person as I introduce.

"My son John and his friend." I can't remember her name.

"Sam, who has the carpentry work for you."

"Of course, you know Dennis, you've been writing . . ."

Gary ignores hands outstretched to him, looks blankly at people, lets me lead him around stiffly, brushing and bumping things as he moves. He is too drunk and too nervous. His hand is turning cooler, cold, and I see sweat on his forehead. I sit him down on the sofa between Barbara and Mother. He sinks back crumpling between them, but his knees are close and taut in front of him.

"What did you think of the election results?" Barbara asks.

Gary shrugs and mutters something I don't hear, but his whole body seems to dismiss our failed hopes.

"Now there's a man," Bob says heartily, "who didn't get carried away by wishful thinking!"

Jake eyes him from the window. "Maybe you have a theory about the election."

But Gary is looking blank and paralyzed again. This is all wrong. He is in shock: the sudden change, the excitement, the long bus ride, the drinking, the sudden confrontation of all these people.

Someone turns up the television. Bless them, they understand. No one is looking at Gary anymore. He sits folded up behind his knees, between squirming Barbara and stiff Mother. I could almost laugh at the picture they make. Mother made a great space between her and Barbara, and look what came to fill it. "I'm going to bed now," she announces, slowly crosses the room, never turning her head to answer the "Good-nights" that follow her, and disappears down the stairway.

He probably should get some food into himself. I go to the kitchen, fix a plate of cheese and nuts, apple and crackers. Coffee. When I come back in, he looks the same, but his eyes are moving around the room, following the sound of voices, beginning to see the people who are talking. Just the way Mother did. Watching. A muscle in his jaw quivers as I set the plate in front of him and sit down beside him in Mother's place. He looks at the food without interest. He is very white now. Maybe he is going to be sick.

"If you're tired," I tell him, "there's no need to sit here being polite. Whenever you like, just tell me and I'll show you your room."

He doesn't answer, but unfolds himself and stands up. He seems taller, longer, each time I look at him. I stand up with him and lead the way across the room. It's impossible for anyone as big as he is to leave unnoticed, but everyone pretends not to notice him. We go down the stairs past John's and Mother's rooms, down the more narrow stairway to The Dungeon.

"There's a toilet and a wash basin down here, but you'll have to shower in one of the other bathrooms."

He goes past me into the bathroom and shuts the door. I hear him throwing up. I clamp my teeth together to stop myself from retching with him, the way I used to when John or Nancy was sick. Should I leave him? But he might pass out in there. But if he comes out and finds me standing here, he'll feel embarassed, more tense than ever.

I go into The Dungeon and turn on the light. It is ready for him: rush mats on the floor, narrow bed along one wall. It's too short for him. He must be used to beds being too short. My little sewing cabinet sits under the window. I always thought it would make a good desk. The typewriter, chair, lamp. Yes, it looks like a writer's room. I hope he likes it.

The toilet flushes and the door opens. He looks a little better now. No real color in his face, but the dead white look is gone. He must have put his head under the faucet. His hair is wet. A thick lock sticks to his forehead. He lurches into the room but doesn't seem to see anything but the bed. While I am opening my mouth to suggest he lie down, he has already fallen on it. He lies on his stomach, his face turned to the wall, his mouth slightly open. His feet hang over the edge. I cover him with a blanket and turn off the light. I hesitate at the door, then decide to leave it open in case he should call for something.

Yossarian is sitting at the top of the narrow stairway, alert, watchful, waiting for me. "It's all right." He has forgiven me for scolding him and insists that he must watch no matter what I say. I pat his head and we walk past Mother's room. The light is on and the door is open.

"Goodnight, Mother."

"So that's he."

"Yes."

"He's been drinking."

"Yes, I know. I guess he needed to celebrate."

Silence.

"Good night, Mother."

Back upstairs, the talk has entered a new phase, the final phase, the beginning of the end. Jake has come away from the window and taken his place in front of the fireplace, forcing John and his girl to move aside and sit up. Jake is thick and substantial. His thick, white hair bristles with authority above his owlish face. His eyes, behind round, wire-rimmed glasses, look very deep and old and wise. They always did, even when he was young, old and wise and a little cold. He is putting the election into historical perspective. Everyone else is quiet except for Judy, who sits at his feet with John and the girl, humming to herself, making little whispered jokes with the young people. She is taking her revenge for the times Jake silenced her during the evening, saying her opinion was wrong, and why it was wrong. All her movements are saying that he is pompous, cold and irrelevant.

Bob breaks in with a disagreeing comment, then Barbara. Jake's cool analysis is punctuated by the comments of all the others, all except Sam, who never talks much and who looks very sleepy. Jake answers them all, draws them into his little speech, comments on the extent to which they are right and the ways in which they are wrong. Usually I am interested in everything Jake says, in the reactions he brings out of others. But tonight I cannot concentrate on his words. I keep drifting away, thinking of other election nights through the years, wandering among them and finally settling on one, centuries ago, when the house was so crowded no one could move, though the children managed to play tag around us and the blaring television sets, and we drank to Kennedy, to new hope, to ourselves, then joined hands (as many black hands as white) and sang, "We Shall Overcome."

"Well, what's going to happen now?" asks Jake.

That is the signal for the end. Pain has been soothed with words. The latest hope, dead and mourned, has been decently buried. A few jokes are passed, and someone yawns. The yawn travels around the room.

"It's after midnight," says Sam as he gets up and heads for the door. A few minutes later, almost all the rest of them are gone. I start upstairs while Millie is still standing with Bob at the open front door, deep in discussion about school. I have a headache. Will he kiss her goodnight? Will they make plans for their next meeting? Am I a masochist or a fool, going upstairs, leaving them alone. But I have such a headache.

I am in bed with the light out when Bob comes up. I pretend to be asleep. If I talk, my head will burst with the echo of my own voice. I think of Gary's long feet hanging over the edge of the narrow bed. Gary is real, and his freedom is real, and I won that. This is not a night of total defeat. I hold tightly to the victory of Gary and his freedom, I hug it as a child hugs a favorite toy and is lulled to sleep.

* * *

THE RAFT PITCHES forward, back, rolls sideways. Hang on. Feet hanging over the edge, in the water, cold water. Sharks? Pull feet up. No room on the raft. Thirsty. Christ, I'm thirsty. Cold, black water. Don't drink the water. Poison. Hang on. Big wave. Look out. Hang on. Over, over.

Fell off the fucking bunk. God, my head. What time is it? Why is it so quiet? Where the hell am I?

Easy. Heart rattling like a can being kicked around in my chest. Nothing to be afraid of. Just a dream. Not in my cell. Out. Free. In Sally's house, in The Dungeon. I can't remember. Must have hit my head. No. Hangover. Christ, what a hangover. Good. Easy now, up. Sit on the bed. Use both hands to hold my head on. Poor stupid head. Thirsty. I'll go to the bathroom, drink some water, piss, hold my head under some cool water.

I remember that. I went to the bathroom, threw up. Yes, this is the bathroom. Look at that sad son of a bitch in the mirror. What's he grinning about? Never thought I'd be happy to have a hangover, good, solid hard hangover.

I hold my head under the cold water. It pounds. Have to stand upright. Hair wet and slicked back, I look like a corpse. That cold water really makes me need to piss. I sound like a waterfall, it's so quiet here. Emptying, emptying myself. Forgot to raise the seat. No seats where I've been. Have to get used to seats again.

A brand new toothbrush and mint toothpaste. Must be for me. God, I could use the whole tube, get the shit taste out of my mouth. Even that wouldn't do it. What in hell did I drink anyway? I started with beer, I can remember that. What I ended with I'll never know.

I laugh, and the sound stabs my eyes, streaks in hot, burning threads over my head and down my neck. What's this bruise on my cheek?

I remember. I walked in and fell flat on my face. The damned dog ready to chew me up. Everybody watching. All her friends. I meant to surprise her. I meant to stand in the doorway and present the envelope full of letters to her. Then we would shake hands, and sit down together and read the letters all over together, and then celebrate and make plans for how we would publish them, ending with a declaration, a list of non-negotiable demands on this society, starting with abolition of all prisons.

Instead, I fell on my face. In front of everyone. Christ, she must be mad. I bet her husband wanted to take a punch at me. Maybe he did. How did I get down here? Maybe I passed out and they carried me down? No, I stood up and threw up. When they got me down here, then what? They all talked about me, trying to figure out how to get rid of me. That's easy. Call the police, call the probation department. Say I'm no good, and it was all a mistake and they don't want any drunk ex-con in their house.

Back to the bedroom, The Dungeon. A nice room. Little table with a typewriter on it. For me. It's a lousy typewriter, old, almost worse than the one I've been using. That window bothers me. Why? All those leaves rubbing up against it like things crawling in on me? Sunlight coming through all green like I'm under water. Gives me the chills. It's too big. Christ, that's what it is, the damn window's too big. I'm used to those thick walls and narrow, dirty windows, used to seeing the world through slits. A big window scares me. Tough ex-con, I'm scared of a big window.

I could climb out. Climb out, and just go. Then I wouldn't have to face her again. If she starts yelling at me or says she's going to report me to my parole officer...maybe she already called the police. No, she wouldn't do that. I don't know. "It's one thing to write letters to a convice, *BUT*..." that's what all those guys kept saying, and they kept it up even more when they found out I was coming here. Why listen to them, losers, just envious, keep to yourself. But what if they were right? I can almost hear her, "After all I did..." I couldn't stand that.

I can't get the window open more than an inch. She was right about this place, cracks all over, windows won't even open.

I have to go upstairs. I can't sit down here all day. If she yells at me or calls the police, I'll just go. She can't stop me, I'm twice her size. She wouldn't yell. She'd talk soft. She'd tell me I shouldn't hurt myself by drinking. I don't have to listen to that crap. I'll act like nothing happened, nothing. And if she says anything, I'll tell her she can't put any of those phony middle-class liberal standards on me. What do they call it? Puritan Ethic. No, that's work. Bourgois convention. But I'm not sure how to pronounce it.

Hell, let's go.

Stairs are really dark. I'm up to the other bedrooms. This one must be John's, and the old lady sleeps here. Light coming down the upper stairway. It feels like climbing a mountain. The light hurts my eyes.

I remember, that's where they all were last night. There was a fire in the fireplace, and they all stood or sat there looking at me. Nobody here now but the cats, stretched out in the sun. The old lady's out on the deck. She doesn't see me.

There's my stuff by the door. I could just grab it and leave, right out the front door before anybody notices. After a while they'd wonder where I was, but by that time I'd be hellandgone from here. And they'd be glad of it. But then the parole officer would call and he'd have me picked up. If they could find me. Where can I go?

"There you are! Isn't this place a mess? I haven't done a thing to clean up yet. I slept late, first time in ages. Bob and John were already gone when I got up." She's walking away, to the kitchen. "...not much to get up for, like the morning after." She's in the kitchen now. Funny how different she looks from her picture. Older. More than that. Smaller, but harder. In her own house. Running things. "Want some eggs?" I guess I have to follow her to the kitchen, otherwise she'll just yell. "This morning, your first morning, I'll cook your breakfast. After that you're on your own. You do eat eggs?"

I nod and watch her putting things on the stove. The kitchen is full of stuff: cartoons on the walls, news clippings on the refrigerator, spice jars and fruit all over the place, plants on all the window sills. Big windows. Sun hurts my eyes. I walk around and look at things, and she keeps talking. "I found that plant on a vacant lot up the side of the hill. How do you like your eggs? John put up that cartoon, but I don't get it. Did you sleep well?" She has a funny voice, like a little girl, but with a hard edge, driving. She moves fast. Her hands flap like she's just messing things up, but then all of a sudden there's all this food laid out on the table, and it looks good. She pours coffee for herself and waves for me to sit down and eat. Like a command.

She pours a tall glass of milk and sets it in front of me. "This is still the best cure I know for a hangover."

I knew it. I put the fork down. She's going to start with all the tolerant sympathy crap. Then we'll have a long heart-to-heart talk about My Drinking Problem. All right, let's get it over with.

"What's the matter, eggs not cooked enough?"

"No, they're fine." She picks up her coffee and sips it and looks past me, out the window. Her eyes look tired and she has bags under them. A little-girl face with old eyes. Okay, it's a bargain, you don't give me a lecture, and I'll try the milk. I take a sip of it, and before I know it, I've drunk it all. I pour another glass and finish that too. She was right. It feels good. She's smiling at me.

"It's hard for us to talk, isn't it?"

"It's hard for me," I tell her. "Doesn't seem hard for you."

"Oh it is. That's why I'm chattering so stupidly, because it's hard to talk now, hard to say words that mean something. Words were all we had between us before. Now, maybe for now, we've just run out of words."

"Maybe."

"Well . . ." She stands up. ". . . when there's nothing to say, one ought to shut up. I'll go clean up the front room and leave you to eat your breakfast in peace."

Once she's gone, I can eat. I feel ashamed to eat in front of her. Why? She's not better than I am. I can't ever let anyone put that on me again. I'm as good as anyone, whether I am or not. Make sense, stupid.

In five minutes the eggs and toast are gone, and my head feels better. I lean back in the chair. I can hear her humming in the front room. I lean back and I feel my shoulder muscles ache, and I realize how tight I am. How scared I was down there! Scared of a window, scared of Sally. I must be half-crazy to be so afraid, to imagine so many things. I'm safe here. I lean back in the chair and look out the window, clear, open space, clear to The Bay. I have to remember, I'm safe here.

* * *

"*THAT'S* the Meyers' house?" Gary ducks his head through the car window, down, out, up, then pulls his head back in. "I thought you said they lost their jobs because they were too radical."

"That was twenty years ago," I tell him. "They lost their teaching jobs."

"Best thing ever happened to them," says Bob.

"You mean in terms of money," I say.

"With Jake's tax business and Judy's real estate, they've really come up in the world."

I hate Bob's using expressions like come-up-in-the-world. "In spite of themselves."

Bob locks the car and we start up the path. "Truth is, they've fantastic heads for business." Somehow it sounds like one of those veiled anti-semitic remarks, though I know Bob genuinely admires Jake.

"And very generous. There are a lot of good causes they support."

Gary mumbles something. It sounds like, "Conscience money." But he's smiling as he looks up at the house. Maybe I heard wrong. I hope he gets on well with them. Jake and Judy could do so much for him, help him get started in something where it won't matter that he's done time. I just hope he doesn't drink too much.

Jake and Judy stand together in the doorway, their arms around each other. Judy's arm encircles Jake's hip as his arm rests on her shoulder. They are like a great bear and a little squirrel together. But they're not fighting, thank God. This will be one of those evenings when Jake leans back and smiles indulgently while Judy talks, instead of stabbing every bubble she sends up with an icycle of logic. "Hello, hello!"

Judy kisses everyone, including Gary. "My God, you're taller than Jake!" She looks like a kitten trying to climb a pole. Gary doesn't bend. But Judy purses her lips at his unreachable face, and tilts her head to one side, shaking it slightly as she would if he were a little boy who had fallen and hurt his knee. She has already adopted him, the way she adopts anyone under forty. Her little face looks more pushed in and scrunched up as the years go by, yet with all the wrinkles and the white hair, she looks like a little girl mothering dolls and pets. Jake's face, his whole head, sags like an old bear tonight. He is not wearing his glasses. If he puts them on, his eyes will glint and his lips will thin and he will analyze our hopes and prospects and mistakes from a cool distance. But not tonight. Tonight he is the host, making drinks.

Gary has been pushed down onto one of the soft, enveloping sofas, where Judy nests her people, sinks them, all warm and helpless, low enough so she can get at them. I must not laugh. Gary's chin is drawn in as if he is afraid she may gobble him up. But his grin is soft, enjoying her mothering as she holds out a sherry to him, like a bowl of chicken soup. Only his eyes are sharp as they dart around the room taking an inventory of objects.

The Meyers' house is bare and exquisite, all beautiful woods and tiles. No messy rugs or animals or drapes because of Jake's allergies. Fine sculpture and paintings. All by local artists, all chosen with Jake's perfect taste, surrounding Judy's bosomy furniture. Jake must have done as much to support some good, starving artists as he has to support political causes. Of course, with his taste, he cannot help making money even in that—some of these things are beginning to be worth a lot of money.

I like being here. It rests me. So unlike the messy house we live in. A cool, clear life. When they're not quarreling.

Judy on her knees on the sofa, leaning forward to hear what Gary is saying. I can't hear him. Bob and Jake standing in front of the fire, just beyond them, in their usual push-pull conversation. Bob is fascinated by Jake's tax business and wants to talk about that; Jake refuses, pulling the conversation back to politics, teaching, unionizing. A struggle of mutual interest in each other's work. Jake should have been able to go on teaching, and I should have let Bob become a businessman.

"How's the Food Project?"

When Jake asks a question, he really wants to know. "The trouble is," I tell him, "it's not just a question of serving a free meal every day, though that's quite a job in itself. The people who come there need everything else besides a free meal: counseling, jobs, clothes, shelter, bus fare home (if we can get them to go), love." I shrug. "Medical care. Some of those kids are so sick by the time they get here they're almost delerious."

"How many do you serve in a day?"

I try to give him clear facts and figures. He listens intently, interrupts me with questions when I go off into personal stories. If I were talking to Judy, I would tell her about the little fourteen year old pregnant girl from Iowa. That's what she would want to hear about. But Jake scowls at such stories. He wants facts. All the facts. And when I'm through giving all the facts I know, I can be sure that tomorrow's mail will bring a large check for the Food Project.

My voice falters as I see Gary reach for the sherry bottle a fourth time. Damn. He sees me watching him. He has a right to relax, to celebrate being free. But how long does the celebration last? I wonder if I should talk to him about it.

Oh, no. He's started telling that story again. This must be the fourth time I've heard it. Jake has stopped listening to Bob. Bob stops talking.

"The visiting room was a sort of a big, long room, painted yellow, with couches and chairs, to make it look homey. Which it couldn't in a million years, no matter what they did. It still smelled prison, if you know what I mean." He shrugs to let us know we can't possibly know what he means. "I never used it. I never had any visitors. The only time I was ever in there was when I had to clean it.

"This one day it was really packed. It was a holiday, Mother's Day, I think. Packed and quiet. You know, after people say hello, what is there to say? They sit and look at the yellow walls. Then somebody asks a question, gets an answer, then it's quiet again. I was cleaning the window and thinking I was glad I didn't have to try to think of something to say to a visitor.

"There were a few kids there. That's a help, because people can watch the kids and say how cute they are, and give them a toy and watch them play with it, and talk about that. This little two-year-old boy was there with his mother. His father was in there only a few months, hadn't seen the kid since he was put in.

"The kid was playing with this little truck, it was a green truck with a cement mixer on it. He was rolling it back and forth and the mother and father were sitting there watching, back and forth, back and forth. Then the kid stopped rolling the truck and just sat there, quiet, like the parents. That happens to most of the kids. After a while, they just stop running around or playing, and they just sit there. Sometimes they start crying.

"This kid just sat looking at his father, puzzled, like he wasn't sure who he was. Then the father held out his arms to the kid. The kid frowned for a minute and held back. Then he seemed to remember. He smiled and put his arms out for his father to pick him up.

"It all happened so fast, I couldn't stop it. First the father held him, stood up, then suddenly he had him by the heels, and he jumped over to the window where I was working, and swung the kid, hard as he could, against the bars on the window. I could hear the bones crack. I tried to grab the guy, but he swung the kid at me like a baseball bat, hit me on the head, then swung him again against the bars.

Then I managed to tackle him, and another prisoner and the guard piled on. We held him down while the guard grabbed the kid and ran to the hospital. But it was no use. The kid died a few hours later.

"Funny thing was, the mother was still sitting there. She hadn't moved. And everyone forgot her in all the excitement. Later somebody noticed her sitting there, and they led her away. I think they had to put her away someplace. Both of them, I guess, they put away somewhere.

"But the worst thing about it was that I could understand it. Do you know what I mean? I mean it didn't seem strange to me. I could see why he wanted to grab the kid and kill him quick as he could. I could see he did it because he loved him. That scared me, scared me more than seeing him do it. Scared me because my mind had become in tune with his, could think, yes, this might be the best way."

Judy is crying, clinging to Gary's arm, tears rolling silently down her face. Jake glances at Judy and annoyance thins his lips: the first tiny step is made toward their next quarrel. Gary has told the story well, improving it through rehearsal with us. Bob glances at me to see how I am taking this.

At the same time, Gary turns his eyes toward me. "Things like that I couldn't put in my letters to you. They would never have got through." His face is flushed, and his speech slurred.

"Then you've a store of things saved up for your books," says Jake. His voice is firm and cool, effectively putting aside such stories as unfit for cocktail hour talk, suggesting to Gary their proper place, yet, I'm relieved to see, not condemning Gary for chilling the evening with such a story. "You're an Ancient Mariner."

Gary shakes his head. "I don't get it. I haven't read that. There's a lot I haven't read."

"Then there are all the more delights in store for you." Jake puts on his glasses but looks thoughtful rather than severe. "The Ancient Mariner." He continues to nod and look at Gary, just for a few seconds. I have seen him look this way as he listens to a piece of modern music, the sort of music that must be patiently suffered until one can be sure whether it is to be "learned up to," as Jake often says, or dismissed as pretentious junk. "Are you free Friday to tackle this place? There's a dead tree needs to be dug out, and some weeding."

"Sure."

Jake turns to Judy. "Well, do you think our vegetarian feast is ready?" Judy jumps up happily, not a trace of tears left. "Judy used

88

you as the excuse to buy two new cookbooks,'' Jake explains. He smiles indulgently and takes off his galsses.

Gary stands up. He is an inch or two taller than Jake and like a pole beside him. Jake throws an arm around Gary's shoulder and takes him ahead of us toward the dining room. I can't see Gary's face. Is he smiling back at Jake or scowling the way he does when one of us touches him? "Did you know Thoreau was a vegetarian?'' Gary's head shakes, no. "And Shaw, and Upton Sinclair, and Shelley . . .''

"And Hitler,'' Bob murmurs as he takes my arm and leads me to the table.

* * *

WHAT WOKE ME? Front door. Television still on, blank and buzzing.

"Oh.'' It's John. He looks at me, at the television.

"What time is it?''

He shrugs. "Three, four.'' He goes into the kitchen and turns on the light. That's all we have to say to each other. We hate each other's guts, probably, I'm not sure yet.

I'm stiff, cold. Mouth dry. I could go to bed. Might as well. Stay out of his way. Thirsty. I go to the kitchen door. He's at the refrigerator. Light hurts my eyes. I go to the sink, fill a glass of water and drink it. I'm hungry. I didn't feel like eating at dinner time, but now I could eat. He's sitting at the table with bread and cheese. He looks up at me, points to the cheese. Okay. I sit down at the table opposite him. We chew.

"Don't you ever sleep?''

"I was asleep when you came it.''

"I mean, like, don't you ever go to bed.''

I shake my head. "Not to sleep.'' I smile and look to see if he got it, but I can't tell. He's very cool. That limp cool doesn't show anything. "I hate going to bed at a certain time, waking up a certain time. When I'm sleepy, I can just fall asleep, any time, any place. No more lights out at ten o'clock.''

He's quiet a minute, just nodding his head. I had a toy like that once, a clown with a big smile. I'd shake him and he'd wiggle all over on springs, then after he was all through wiggling, his head would keep nodding up and down, up and down.

"Guess you don't ever want anyone telling you what to do and what time to do it any more."

He means the time I spent at The Farm. I shake my head. "No, I was always that way. When I was a little kid I was afraid I wouldn't wake up. It's like dying, going to bed all wrapped up in sheets." Why did I say that to him? Now I'm going to get that look, the one I've gotten all my life, the look that says, you're weird, man.

But he just keeps nodding, like he's saying, yes, that's the way you feel. I hate people like that. They hold back their reaction to something, pretending they don't have any reaction. You say something and they just let it sit there like something you spilled on the floor. That's worse than giving me the look.

He gets up, goes to a cupboard under the sink, and comes up with a bottle of wine. He holds it up to me, and I nod, so he gets two glasses and sits down. We don't talk while he opens it and pours it. We don't talk while we drink the first glass. We just let it slip down and do its work, warm and easy. He fills the glasses again. Then he nods again, as if I said something, just three or four slow nods.

"You don't sleep much either," I tell him. Except for election night, he's been out this late every night.

He nods. "Yeah, but I go some place. You sit around here like my grandmother all day."

"Yeah, we do our knitting together."

That cracks him up. He opens his mouth wide and this little scratching, high laugh comes out. He shakes his head and pours another glass. "You and my grandmother sitting together, knitting." It wasn't that good, but we laugh some more anyway. "Well, why don't you?"

"Why don't I what?"

"Go somewhere. Go out. You're free now, man."

"I haven't got a car."

He looks at me for a minute. "There's a bus stop up the corner from here."

I shrug. "Go where? Where is there for me to go around here? I don't know anyone. I don't . . .''

He's nodding again and frowning. He looks like his father, pug nose and red cheeks. But his face is thin and long, like his hair, so his color looks like a flush, like the TB flush my uncle had just before he died. "Sure, I just thought you'd go crazy cooped up in here, like you'd be pacing up and down or going out and walking around the block.''

"There's no place to walk.''

His frown goes deep. He doesn't know what I mean. He looks at my eyes and waits.

"Out there." I make a little wave toward the window. "It's so empty.''

"Empty?''

"No people, no stores or bars or . . . it's dead out there, nothing but up and down, tripping over treeroots.''

He's still frowning but after a minute he nods again, very slowly this time. "I used to pump my bike up to the top of the hill and then coast down. It was like flying.''

Bike. He means a bicycle. With pedals. Now there's the difference between us. The great gulf. "Well, I guess you had to do something to feel alive on this street.''

Now he nods with comprehension, emptying the bottle into our glasses. "Yeah, not growing up on a real street, like you did." He's not so bad. "My father grew up there. But he hated it.''

"Well, your father is . . . something else.''

For a minute we're silent, looking at our glasses. Then both at once, we burst out laughing and drain the glasses. He gets up and opens another bottle. "My father," he says as he sits down, "didn't want me to grow up on the streets he knew. He wanted me to be with the trees and fresh air up on the hill. Right? Right. At the same time, he's a liberal so I have to go to public school. That's democracy. Down the hill." He makes a little down-swoop motion with his flat hand. "Down the hill every day . . . to those other streets.''

I take another gulp, then let him have it. "Is that why you quit high school? Cause you were scared?''

But he doesn't get mad. He just gives me the slow nod again. "Of guys like you.''

We smile at each other, leaning over the table, our faces close. He can admit he's afraid of something, and it doesn't bother him at all, doesn't shame him. Nothing shames him, I think. I don't know if I like him, but I like him admitting he was afraid. So I say, "Sure, I was a real tough guy, and look where it got me." He nods, and we seem to be on an even plane for a minute. Equals. Even friends. It must be the wine. I reach for the bottle and pour another glass. "I bet you did things as bad as I did and never got locked up.''

He nods more and more. "I stole a car once. A neighbor's. They were as embarrassed as if they'd done something wrong."

I feel myself going hot. "A precious, protected member of the middle class."

". . . and look where it got me," he says, imitating me.

I look around. "It got you here, where you were born. Not so bad."

He looks around like he hates the place. "The little nest, where I can always come back if it gets too tough out there. Trouble is it's always too tough out there, and when it gets scary, I can come back. So I'm almost twenty-five years old and still in mother's bosom."

"There's worse places you could be."

He doesn't answer, or even nod this time. He pours some more wine and drinks the whole glass down, so I do the same thing.

"But . . ." He points his finger at me. A familiar gesture. Yes, that's what his father does when he wants to make a point. But it looks funny, because John's finger is a little limp. ". . . I have plans."

"You mean studying math at the junior college."

"Right!" His voice barks sharp and loud, like it was suddenly someone else's voice. He points his finger at me again. "And that is the difference between a failure and a success. I am a success because I am making it possible for my parents to say, when asked, that I am a student of Computer Science. They are *so* grateful for my providing them with this answer, at least for a while, when their friends ask what in hell I'm doing."

We laugh and raise our glasses in a toast. The finger he points is getting stiffer, he's sitting up straighter. He's stopped nodding like a spring toy.

"You too should come to the college, take on the magic title of Student."

"Yeah, I'm supposed to."

"When?"

I shrug and then before I know it I'm saying, "When I stop being too scared to walk out of this house." I almost shout it. Like gunshots. Then I laugh. "I tell you, all those trees out there, all that empty space, it scares the shit out of me. And the goddamn dogs. I'll either get chewed up by one of them or slip on a pile of dog shit and break my ass."

Now he really laughs, not that shivery giggle, a big bellow that makes me laugh with him.

"Have you always been like this?"

"Scared? Yeah, well, no. Not scared to go out, not like this. No, this is something new."

He nods, short and jerky, once. "Zo." He empties the bottle into our glasses. "You have come to zee right doktor. I veel take you veeth me to zee college." He pulls on an imaginary beard and leans forward. "Vee veel not let zee trees get you!"

We touch our glasses.

"Tomorrow!" he says.

"Tomorrow!"

We drain our glasses and start laughing again.

"Don't you two realize that people are trying to sleep!" Sally is in the doorway. She is wrapped in a faded blue robe and her eyes are like slits. Her face sags, angry and mean and old. "Do you know it's after four o'clock? If you're going to stay up all night, the least you could do is be quiet!"

She wheels around and is gone. I hear her going up the stairs. She is really mad, at John, at me. Maybe more at me. Thinks I've corrupted her son, keeping him up late drinking. No, he's always up late anyway. But she's mad. I could see the way she looked at the two of us. John and me together. Two against one.

Funny, that gives me a kind of satisfaction. I put that look on her face. I had the power to shake up the mind behind those tired eye slits. It felt good. For just a minute. Now I feel a cold blast, like she chilled the whole kitchen.

I look at John. He is still smiling, and he has started nodding again. He is satisfied too. Satisfied with what? I wish I wasn't so drunk, so I could think, so I could figure out why he looks so satisfied. Like he won one round in a long match. A fight I don't know anything about. Some fight going on between him and his family, forever. Something I just walked into, ignorant, stupid, just walked into and got used. That's how I feel. Like I've been used.

We both stand up, and he grins and whispers, "Tomorrow." Then we take off our shoes and go down the steps. fairly quietly, him first. He goes into his room and closes the door without looking back at me. And I go on alone down to The Dungeon.

* * *

"SO THEN he accused *me* of taking advantage of *him*! And he didn't even change the tire." Suddenly Barbara laughs. At herself. "Anyway, that's over. I stuffed his things in his rucksack and put it outside the garage door. He can find some place else to park it."

I glance at the clock. Nearly noon. The co-op will be a madhouse by this time and I have that Save-The-Bay meeting at one. She sees me looking at the clock.

"I'm sorry. I guess you had more important things to do on a Saturday morning than listen to my problems . . ."

"Nothing is more important than . . ."

". . . but I don't know what I'd do if I couldn't talk to you." She guesses what I'm thinking. "No, No, I wouldn't do anything like that again. You can count on it. I hope you're not listening to me because you're afraid of that."

"I'm listening to you because we're friends."

"You don't know what it's like."

"No." I can't imagine. If I were alone. If I told Bob to leave, if I made him choose between me and Millie and he chose her, what would it be like? Would I become like Barbara? With long earrings and long hair and a skirt slit up the side?

"What are you smiling about?"

I shake my head.

"Well, it is funny, a woman my age getting mixed up with these twenty-five-year-old freeloaders. They're all alike, don't think I haven't seen the pattern." She tosses her long hair. Her earrings and her breasts sway. She is so pretty, so attractive, except for the haunted, empty look in her eyes. "Oh, I'm so sick of sex," she murmers. "I'm so sick of men."

"If you see this pattern," I say, cautiously, "couldn't you break it?"

She laughs. "Sure. Sure, I break it every day, the way some people quit smoking. Hundreds of times. And then I'm alone . . ."

I've started her off again. I don't need to listen to the words now. I think of Barbara as she was when I met her. Beautiful, in a cotton print dress, with her two beautiful girls and her handsome husband. What a wonderful cook she was, a fine pianist, a mainstay in Women for Peace. What happened? What blew it all apart? And when it came apart, why should she be the one to suffer so much? It isn't fair.

94

"Anyway, I'm having a fine damned time!" That bit of bravado means she's coming to the end now. "Can you imagine the way I lived five years ago, driving the girls to ballet lessons and doing the pipe and slippers routine with George?" I nod that, yes, I can imagine it, but she doesn't notice. "And, God how bored and miserable I was underneath all that, wondering, is this all there is? is this what I worked so hard for? How I hated it all, how ashamed I was of hating it. Whatever happens, I'm better off now than I was then."

That's probably true. Whatever sad and ugly metamorphosis she is going through now, who am I to say whether she might not be becoming a better woman?

"That's what I like about you, Sally, you don't judge. And that means I end up telling you all this squalid junk. Do you know what Maureen said to me?"

"Oh, is Maureen in town?"

She nods. "For the holidays. I invited her and Jack and the baby to stay with me and she said, 'Oh, Mother, thanks, but your house is so messy, and a baby needs a clean environment."

"Maureen?!"

We both laugh, remembering how Maureen stumbled around in filthy rags, stoned on dope throughout her sixteenth year, then announced she was pregnant. She waited a long while afterward to add that she intended to marry the father and that he was a very high-salaried accountant.

"Oh, hi!"

I follow her glance and see that Gary is standing in the doorway, yawning. He nods soundlessly and makes that funny little smile of his. It is the smile of a man who has just had surgery, forgets and laughs, and the laugh turns into a grimace of pain.

He goes into the kitchen and comes back with a cup of coffee. He sits down on a chair opposite the sofa where we sit. Since that first day when I cooked his breakfast he has eaten nothing but pots of coffee all day, then wine in the afternoon, till dinner. So what, I'm not his mother.

"Anyway my daughters have turned out super-respectable, in reaction, I'm sure, to what they consider their mother's total degeneration!" She looks at Gary as she laughs, but he is looking at Yossarian, who sits in the corner looking back at him. "You and that dog make friends yet?" Gary shakes his head. "Well, he's Sally's dog, dogged devotion and all that." Gary makes no effort at the smallest smile. He seems to grow more morose every day. Maybe it's because he just sits around the house all day. He doesn't even read. "When are you coming with your trusty machete to hack a path through my jungle?"

Bless Barbara. Whatever her own problems, she hasn't forgotten her promise.

Gary shrugs. "Tuesday?"

"Good. Look, I might be out till about four, if I get work that day. Whenever you get there, just start hacking away at the shrubs and grass in the back yard. Tools are in the garage. I'll leave the back door open in case you . . ."

"Oh, should you do that?" I warn her.

She shrugs. "Never can remember to lock anything. Haven't much that's worth taking anyway." She stands up. Her jewelry makes a little clinking noise. "Must go. Well, thanks for listening, as we used to say in the golden days of radio."

I walk with her to the front door, and, as she turns to say goodbye, I see the hunted look in her eyes again, as if she is going out again to a threatening world. As, of course, she is. I close the door behind her, feeling helpless and useless. Gary looks at the front door. His look is ugly.

"Barbara is a very old and dear friend." I don't know why I said that or what it is supposed to mean.

A look of total contempt comes over his face. "A lot older than she'd like to be."

I feel myself go hot, and I open my mouth to defend her. But Gary doesn't notice. He has turned back to face Yossarian. "Some babe, eh, Yossarian."

"Please don't talk about her that way." My voice sounds much more stern and cold than I meant it to sound, and I realize I am much more angry at Gary than I thought I was. I start to tell him about Barbara, insisting that he listen and understand. But how can he understand? He is so young.

"So now she collects alimony and plays hippie. Over-the-hill-hippie." It is the first time I've heard Gary laugh, a short, stuttering, choked sound.

"No! You've got it all wrong. She worked to put her husband through college. She waited on tables, all through his med school. While he was getting established, she worked in his office, even

96

though she was already having babies. Then, just when they began to be secure, and she could slow down, he ran off with a nineteen-year-old patient. She used the alimony to go back to school. Now the girls are gone, there's no more alimony. She substitute-teaches in the Oakland schools—where she can find work because so many other people are afraid to go there. She's alone. Nothing but that house. Why, even you have more than she has—people who care about you, a place to come home to where people . . . ." I've been shouting. How stupid. Pacing up and down and shouting. I sit down on the sofa, facing him. "I'm sorry, Gary, I didn't mean to shout at you. It's just that I feel so . . . ."

He smiles. It's rather a nice smile this time. It doesn't go all crooked. "It's all right. You're loyal to your friends. All your friends. Even a dumb old broad who . . . all your friends." He nods. He keeps nodding.

I'm very tired. It's after one. No time left to Save the Bay.

"You're mad."

I shake my head and take a deep breath. As I let it out I wonder if I am angry at Gary. "It's just that . . . Gary, you are so very critical of people, of things, since you came. I guess I expected . . . oh, not gratitude, not all that false feeling." His face has stiffened, then relaxed a little. But it is still stiff. It is hard for him to take criticism. Hard for all young people. I must remember that. "I thought you would be . . . more tolerant. Because you have seen, have lived with people who have . . . had trouble. You . . . you're so hard on Barbara."

I wait for him to answer. Other times, in the past few days, when he won't talk, I just go on chattering in desperation, but this time I wait. I will sit here and wait all day until I force him to answer me.

"There's . . . a lot of bitterness left in me."

"Bitterness, yes, that I can understand. Bitterness toward people who hurt you. But Barbara never hurt you, she's incapable of hurting anyone but herself. You judge her so harshly . . . the way my mother does." I wait even longer this time.

"I guess . . . it's because she has everything. She . . . you . . . all of you . . . people have money and security and . . . Barbara may think she's poor but she doesn't know what poverty is."

"Granted, but that doesn't explain the dislike you've taken to her. You have, haven't you?"

He shakes his head, no, but shrugs a kind of yes.

"But you've known people with just as messed-up lives. You wrote to me that you did."

"Yes, but they had reasons. What's her excuse?"

"Gary," I tell him, "you mustn't think we're anything but human beings, just like you."

He doesn't answer. He gets up and goes to the kitchen. I hear him pouring more coffee. After a while I look through the doorway and I see him standing at the window, looking out and slowly sipping his coffee.

* * *

I'M NOT HUNGRY. The wine and nuts filled me up. But just because it's six o'clock, we have to sit here and eat. That look Sally gave me when she went to the refrigerator to take out the wine and found it was gone, a dead soldier on the sink, then telling Bob to open a new bottle. Big ceremony he goes through with a cork screw.

I used to wonder what it would be like. All my life, when I saw it in movies or on television, a family around the dinner table, all eating together, every day, the same time. What a lot of crap. I don't want to sit at the table with a bunch of people, whether I'm hungry or not, whether I want to see them or not, just because it's six o'clock. I might as well be locked up if I have to do something like that.

I wonder if it's always like that. You see other people have something you don't have, and you want it. You use up years wanting it. Then you get it, and you find out you don't want *that*. Maybe you can have anything you want when you stop wanting it. No. There's so much I want and I can't stop wanting, I could never stop wanting, but what is it I want? Not this. Everything I look at here, I think, no, not this, not that. Then what do I want?

"The salt, Gary. Please, pass the salt?"

"Huh? Sure." It slips out of my hand, funny little round thing like a rough rock. Never saw a salt shaker like that before. Probably something Sally made.

". . . for the reading lab," Bob says. You can tune in and out on him all the time without missing a thing. Whatever he says, it's all the same.

"Ridiculous name," says Sally. "Makes me think of books in test tubes. I thought reading had something to do with books."

Bob laughs. That gave him just the opening he needed to start talking about all that machinery again.

"Now I know what's familiar about you."

Bob looks at me, confused. He's lost his thought and doesn't know what I mean. But he picks up what I said, pretends to be interested. "What?"

"The way you talk."

Bob laughs. "You mean my Mission District accent. When I was in the marines people used to take me for a New Yorker—Brooklyn. Same ethnic mix, I guess, Irish, Italian, Jewish. You don't have it. I guess the mix is changing."

He sounds like that coach at Horace Mann Junior High School who used to kick me in the ass because he couldn't get me to go out for basketball. Looks like him too, pug-nose, thick jaw, big round eyes. He talked all the time too. God, he never stopped talking, about how we could all be Mission Bums or we could amount to something if we did what he said. And end up like him, teaching Mission Bums all day. I said that to him once and he hit me. He knew how to do it without leaving any marks.

"They're the coming thing. That's what I'd like to get into. I'm thinking of proposing it for my sabbatical next year. A complete study of electronic devices for the teaching of reading. There's money coming in for that now. Then, when I get back, with my sabbatical report, I'll be the logical one to set up the new lab." He goes on talking, sounding more and more like a salesman trying to sell me a machine.

"Oh, it just seems to me that there's always money for gimmicks."

"Sally, you have to move with the times. The kids expect sophisticated approaches to . . ."

"Sophisticated! Those toys?"

"No, Dad's right," says John. "Books are such a bore."

They look at him. He's looking down at his plate. Then they look at each other.

"Anyway that's what the funds are earmarked for, and there's a lot more coming if we can present a good proposal."

"A lot more coming, for gadgets, machines, junk that will be bought and played with, passing the time pretending to solve problems no one knows how to solve."

"Well, what do you expect . . ."

"I'd expect you to have more intelligence than the administrators who buy those gimmicks."

"I don't decide what . . ."

"Maybe you should. Maybe that's what you should be working on in the union, instead of trying to get yourself a soft berth in the . . ." She spits out the words. ". . . reading lab!"

Bob talks a lot, but he doesn't finish a sentence very often. Sally's so far ahead of him she knows what he's going to say before he does, and answers before he finishes saying it.

Tune out, have some more wine. Where did it all go? I guess I've been hitting it pretty steady. John watches me pour out the last few drops. Can't think of a better way to get through these happy family dinner hours.

I'm not the only one who feels this way. The old lady sits there looking like we all smell bad. I don't think she hates me any more than the rest of them. Look, old lady, you and I have something in common. We both think Bob is a phony and John is a freeloader, and we're both sick of talking about saving the world at the dinner table every night. Poor John, you've been listening to this all your life. Maybe that's what's wrong with you. I could almost feel sorry for you.

No.

No, because you can just get up from the table and walk away, which is what you're going to do in few minutes. Unless you just jump in and talk about yourself. That'll shut up your mother and father. They'll shut up and listen and look worried and hope that if they listen hard and long enough you'll finally say something that'll give them hope you're not going to freeload on them till you're seventy. Or the old lady will give a big sigh and start off, "When your father was . . ." and go into some long, stupid story about The University in the old days, and everyone will listen or pretend to listen, at least keeping quiet for a change. The old lady is the only one who never gets interrupted.

And I'm the only one who has nothing to say. I'm the only one who has to sit here keeping my elbows off the table (hell, why not put my elbows on the table? There!) and listening and pretending to be interested because what right have I to say anything—what have I got to say anyway? I'm here to get assimilated into this high-class life, this place where people sit around a table at the same time every night and argue out the world's problems and show each other how much

100

they're doing to solve them. I'm just one of the problems they are solving. I'm just here to prove they really are solving them. The only thing I can do is remember to use my napkin and . . . oh, Christ, not spill my glass of wine. That was the last of it, and I bet she won't open another bottle.

"Pour salt on it."

"Never mind."

"Want some lamb, Gary? Oh, I forgot."

"I wouldn't eat that stuff if you paid me a million dollars," I tell John. I see Sally looking at the plate of beans and rice she fixed for me. I'm not eating that either, she's thinking.

"Why not?"

"The human digestive tract wasn't made to handle flesh. Think about that. Our ancestors were all herbivorous. The flesh you eat putrifies in your gut. Not only that, but it's full of additives that cause cancer." Now they are all quiet, listening to me. This must be the first time I've said anything at the dinner table. The first time I've had any contribution to make. The list of additives. Once I memorized them. Nothing else to do, I lay on my bunk and I memorized the list of additives in meat. Beautiful words. Now I rattle them off.

John starts his nodding act again. "You an expert on nutrition?"

"I had plenty of time to become an expert." Then I pick up where I left off. They're not listening. They're just being polite. Why don't they just jump in and change the subject the way they do with each other? No, they're giving me special treatment. They're condescending to listen to the ex-con's esoteric knowledge, encouraging him to feel like a part of the family, this polite, lying family. That's what it is. Being polite is lying, pretending something's all right with you when it isn't. Bob watches me and nods, and then reaches for his third helping of meat. I feel like I could shoot out my arm across the table and knock it off his plate.

"Not eating meat is supposed to make people non-violent," says Sally. "Is that true?"

Hell, I don't know, but I'm not going to admit that now. I nod my head. "There's plenty of times I would have lost control, probably killed somebody, in that place, if I hadn't quit eating flesh, if I didn't have my gut in tune with my reason. But dietary purification is the first step in . . ." I'm making it all up as I go along. They're all watching me, not moving, not even eating anymore, but I can't read the expressions on their faces. My head is starting to hurt. The cords in the back of my neck are pulling tight again. I feel like they know I'm faking it.

I stop talking.

I reach for the bottle of wine, then remember it's empty. Sally reaches for the plate of lamb, then stops and draws back her hand.

"Hey, is that the right time?" Bob jumps up. "I have to go."

Sally's still looking at the plate. "I thought the meeting wasn't till eight."

"It isn't. I have to pick someone up."

Sally doesn't answer. She just keeps looking at that plate of dead flesh.

*　*　*

"MRS. MORGAN?" He looks uncertain, standing there in the doorway, as if he has come to the wrong house, or as if he is a brand new salesman, too shy to sell whatever he has to offer.

"Yes. Are you Mr. Raymond from the Probation Department?"

He nods, looks relieved but still shy and confused. I motion for him to come in.

"My sister lives up here and I was going to her place for dinner tonight, so when I saw your address was so close . . ." He is a small, neat black man. His suit is shiny, light blue and his tie is bright red. He wears thick-soled shoes, to make him look taller? Shoes shiny bright, face shiny bright. Dapper. Do people use that word anymore?

"Do you want to . . . inspect the house?"

He looks embarrassed. "Oh, no." He swings around in a half circle as if taking in everything. "It's all . . ." He shrugs apologetically. "Just a routine . . . not necessary to . . ." He leaves sentences half-finished in the air as he pivots on one foot, as if to make a quick getaway. He stops as he sees Gary sitting at one end of the sofa reading the newspaper. Gary does not look up at him. Slowly he turns a page.

"Wilson?"

"Yes, this is Gary," I say.

Gary looks up. His fact is blank and taut. The black man's hand twitches as if he would bring it forward, offering to shake hands, but he changes his mind as he sees Gary's expression.

"I'm Mel Raymond," he says. "I'll be your parole officer. You were supposed to check in at the Oakland office. Didn't they tell you?"

Gary doesn't answer, just looks at him over the top of the newspaper, as if waiting for him to finish talking so that he can go back to reading the paper. This is silly. It takes me back to the days when the truant officer used to come to the house, and John would sit there, defying the man to pick him up and carry him back to school.

"I haven't had a chance to go through your file yet." He turns to me. "My case load is unbelievable." Then he makes a little half swing around again, taking in me and the house. "You're a lucky man." He smiles at Gary's rigid face, then turns round to finish the smile at me. "Certainly in good hands here."

There is a silence, and I don't know quite how to fill it. "Is there anything I should . . ."

Now he looks a bit official. "You have a statement of the conditions of parole?" I nod. "He's to report in to the office in Oakland within the next week. I'll visit or call every few weeks. Probably call. I've got a case load you wouldn't believe." The silence falls again and he looks annoyed. "I hope," he says to Gary, "you know what a lucky man you are to be here. Not very many parolees can come out to a place like this."

Gary looks even more stiff. There's a little muscle near his jaw that quivers. The newspaper quivers at the same time. I wish the man would stop saying how lucky Gary is.

"You got it made, man." His smile is broad and false. His little effort at being cozy fails, and the smile fades. He turns back to me. "As long as he stays here and stays out of trouble, you probably won't see me again. With the caseload I've got, I'm lucky to keep up with emergencies. Of course, if you ever want to call me, if there's a problem . . ." He holds out his card to me, and I take it. Now he is talking as if Gary isn't here, as some people talk in front of children. That's worse. But it was Gary who closed him out. Gary has pushed the newspaper up again, and his face is hidden. "Now that's a very interesting painting." He is working his way toward the front door. "Who is the artist?"

"Oh. I did that."

"You did?" He is impressed but not as much as he pretends to be. I feel like a child being praised for a recitation. "And you play piano too?" He motions towards the old upright where I've left the music in the usual mess. I nod. Then I hope he won't do it again, but he does. He turns once more toward Gary and says, "You're a lucky man. Make the most of it." I can't wait to get the front door open, then closed behind him. My jaw feels tight and sore from the false smile I put on it. I realize my teeth are clenched and I let my jaw fall.

I feel guilty as I walk back into the room, looking at the newspaper still held in front of Gary's face. The newspaper is not lowered. He keeps it up between us. I don't blame him if he is offended. "That was stupid," I say. How do I tell him how I hate discussing him as "a case" without making it all worse? I laugh. "I felt like a little girl called to the principal's office."

From behind the newspaper he says, "You didn't sound like it."

"Oh. What did I sound like?"

He lowers the newspaper and makes a little half-circling gesture, imitating the gesture of the dapper little man. "Like the Lady Of The House."

The gesture is funny but his imitation takes in me too. "Well, you didn't help much. You left me to do all the talking."

"What was I supposed to do when he kept telling me how lucky I am, say yessir, yes master, yes, I sure am a lucky man, sir, and I sure do promise to be a good little boy and not disappoint my benefactress, The Lady Of The House."

Now he is behind the newspaper again.

"You're right. That was awful." I start straightening up the music on the piano. I always forget to close one piece of music before opening another, so there are opened books layered everywhere, and when I sit down to play, I can't find a thing. "Still, he wasn't bad. Seems a shy, nice sort of man. Not at all what I expected." I hear a furious crackling of paper and turn to see that Gary has slammed the newspaper down on his lap, crushing it and ripping it in his clenched fists.

"Shit!"

That's the first time he has sworn in front of me. That's good. I'm sure he's been too shy to talk in his normal way, the normal way for all young people now. I've gotten used to young girls sounding like army sergeants. I'm glad he's feeling at home enough to say shit. But I wish he wouldn't look at me so angrily.

"That guy tiptoes around this place like it was a shrine. The shrine of the middle class. He's so impressed he doesn't know what to do. He has to tell you his sister lives up here, so you know he's no low class nigger, no, sir, he's one of you, and I'm white trash, lower than any nigger.''

I wish he wouldn't use that word. Twenty years ago Bob threw out a man who used that word in this house, and it hasn't been used here since. "Of course, he's a snob," I say, "but I don't see why you're so angry . . .''

He throws the newspaper to the floor. The paper is so badly damaged, just from his one gesture, as if great hands had crunched and shredded it. I can't imagine how one movement did that much damage. It's as though his fury alone made the paper shrivel and tear itself. "You think he acts that way in the houses of other parolees?" He stands. Every time he gets up I'm surprised at how long he is . . . not tall, because he slouches, but long. "He was really out of his element here. He didn't know how to act. He cringed around, then got out fast. Didn't know what to do here! Why? Cause he's used to walking into houses like the people who live there are shit, that's why. He's used to sniffing around like everyone smells bad. He's used to feeling like his fifty-dollar shoes are the best thing ever walked into a house. And he's used to people looking at him like they agreed with him, because if they don't . . .''

"I don't know, Gary, I can only judge by what he does here, and I didn't see anything really offensive in his manner . . .''

"You wouldn't. You never will. You'll never know what I'm talking about, why I hate those guys, because you're middle-class, with your home on the hill . . .''

"It's your home now too.''

". . . what my probation officer in San Francisco used to do? He'd count the beer cans in the garbage can before he came in, then tell me to stop drinking so much. He'd tell me, why don't you clean this place up? And he never asked what artist painted the pictures on the wall either. He used to scare the shit out of my mother. She was so afraid of him. Christ, she was afraid of any official person—she was afraid of the god-damned mailman! She'd sit wringing her hands and shaking the whole time he was there, and he'd enjoy it. I'm telling you . . .'' He gestures toward the front door. ". . . you put that little smart-ass in the front room of a place in a housing project, and he'll swell up to the size of three men and stomp around like he owns the place. And there's nothing, nothing you can do but sit there, in your own place, and take it. And when I wouldn't take it, when I told him what I thought of him, counting beer cans and scaring my mother, that guy had me put away. You don't believe that, and you'll never believe that, because it never happened to you, because you've never been poor. Unless you know what that means, you don't know anything, you won't ever know anything, you won't believe it because no one ever treated you that way." He seems to fold up, crumple and fall back onto the sofa, defeated, not angry anymore, but tired, disgusted. I would rather see him angry.

I wonder how many people have told Gary how lucky he is to be taken in here. How awful it must be to be told that over and over again. How would I feel if someone said that to me? I must try to imagine it.

Funny. I can't imagine that it would make the slightest bit of difference what anyone said to me. I'd probably agree that I was lucky and forget it. But I can understand that it would make Gary angry. I can understand it, but I can't feel it. Maybe that's what makes him so angry. He wants me to feel the same angry pain he does. But what good would that do?

* * *

"YOU CAN KEEP the tape recorder," Barbara says. "I never use it. It was just one of those expensive toys my ex-husband left behind."

"Thanks." I open the car door. I can feel her looking at me, wondering why I don't look straight back at her. She's wondering why I don't like her, or act like I don't. She gives me smiles and tape recorders and gets all nervous trying to be nice so I'll like her and she won't worry about something being wrong with her because I don't like her. Most people are that way, especially women. With people like that, the cooler you are, the more they want to do for you, to prove they're all right.

"Want to work again this Thursday? Might as well get the jungle cleared."

"Might as well." She leans over to pull the door shut, so I get a flash of breasts under that shirt that's open down to the third button. Women her age should wear a bra. She drives off, and I'm alone in front of Sally's house.

Kid next door left his tricycle out again. Never seen him ride it. Surprised he doesn't roll down the hill and get killed on it. But I'm

106

more surprised just seeing it here. Reminds me of the first time I went along with my mother when she went to clean a house in Pacific Heights, and I saw all those big houses, with big cars and big trees, and I asked her who could live in these big houses. She said if people worked real hard and saved their money, some day they could afford to live in big houses like those. I thought about that, and I imagined all those big houses full of old people who had worked hard and saved their money and now were rich.

Then I saw a tricycle outside one of the houses, in a big driveway, where three cars were parked. I was stunned. I thought, how can those people afford this house already, when they still have small children? They haven't worked long or hard enough to save enough money to get this house. Then I knew she was lying, lying to herself and to me, and that no matter how hard she worked, or I worked, we were never going to have enough money for a house like this. But it still surprises me to see a toy or a little kid playing around a street that has big houses on it.

Well, you can't stand here all afternoon, might as well start hauling yourself up to the house. It's a wonder no one breaks their necks coming down or has a heart attack going up. That's one thing the old lady and I agree on, it should be easier to get into your own god-damned house.

Sally doesn't mind. She takes it slow, even when she's carrying a bag of groceries. She looks at everything along the way, like she's saying hello to her friends. There's the bristlecone pine she got two Christmases ago, there's the laurel she planted when John was three, there's the rock she found at Stinson Beach, there's this and there's that. Little Red Riding Hood on her way through the woods, picking flowers. It's true, now I see, now that she pointed things out to me, there's a lot of stuff, a lot of nice stuff here. Like the little bowls she made that catch the rain and the funny little bird houses hanging cat-safe from a few branches, and that Buddha she drapes flowers on and those purple primroses blooming now, in the wet, in the shadows, like secret things. She acts like I know the names of all these things she's planted. A couple of times she even asked me the names of things she didn't know. How should I know? A tree is a tree. Just because I mentioned a little gardening in my letters, I'm supposed to be an authority. I don't know anything. Wait till she finds out I don't know the things she thinks I know.

You can hardly get to the front door, the porch is so full of pots, house plants out for an airing. Yossarian in there, barking his head off. He knows me, he knows it's me on the porch, but he'll bark all the louder. When Sally gets to the porch, she always turns around and looks at the view before she comes in. It's different every minute, she says. It looks the same to me. Trees and housetops, then only housetops, dark line of smog, water; today you can't even see the water, fog rolling in fast.

"Shut up, Yossarian. You growl at me, I'm going to kick your teeth out one of these days." I didn't start this. I get along all right with animals. But he always acts like I'm going to hurt Sally or something.

Damn door sticks. No door in this house shuts right. It's almost as bad as the old projects. That's the truth. This place is built like crooked bureau drawers stuck halfway out of an old bureau, tipped over from one leg missing (like that old one my mother had I could never get her to throw out) and all the drawers stuffed full of junk. No wonder they got such a bargain. Even twenty, thirty years ago, this place must have been a loser.

Christ, I'm tired. "Anybody home?" The old lady must be down in her room. Good, she won't have to watch me get the wine and a glass and stretch out here. I ought to change these pants or get the mud off them before I lay on the sofa. Oh, the hell with it.

I hate this house. I hate this house. No, I don't. I don't care one way or the other. Why should I hate it? Because it's built so shitty. No, I've lived in worse. Because it's up here, away from everything. Well, it's still closer to everything than I've been for two years. Have another glass of wine. Don't mind if I do. Now. Look around and tell me why you hate this house.

Fireplace, full of ashes and whatever paper anyone throws in, mantel covered with shells, rocks, glass bottles, everything with a story, a history, just ask Sally, no, don't ask her, too late, she'll tell you anyway the minute she sees you looking at it. Painting above, old saw in the back yard on a pile of wood. Sally painted it. Piano in the corner. Sally pounds out Bach every afternoon while dinner is cooking: her therapy, she says. John plays rock by ear and sings. Even Bob picks out three Irish tunes that all sound like Danny Boy.

Bookshelves. Here, in the dining room, in all the bedrooms, halls, even the bathroom, piles of books. They must have never thrown away a book in their lives. I'm tired of Sally, every time I say something, jumping up and saying she's got a book on that and hunting around till she brings it to me, throws it down next to me. Then she rushes off to do something else, and I let the book sit there.

I can't read. I tried. I don't know what's wrong with me, but I just can't read. And she probably thinks that I was lying about all the books I read in prison. She probably has decided I'm a phony, just a low-class illiterate. Sorry she ever asked me to come here. Worst mistake she ever made.

Plants. Every window sill, hanging from the ceiling, sitting on the floor, and she still comes in carrying some little stem or twig to root in water on the window sill above the sink, then "if they take" put in a pot. They always take. All these stems and twigs she gathers growing into a god-damned jungle in the house. Only thing stops them from taking over is that she's always giving them away. Person can't leave this house without taking a plant along. Want it or not, you got a little green friend to take home with you from Sally's house.

Yossarian jumps up when I laugh. "You just stay in your corner, you mean bastard, and I'll stay in mine." This white wine is like water. I'll go out myself and get some red tomorrow.

Stained glass hanging in the window. I never noticed that before. Pretty, the way it turns and catches the sun. Probably something else Sally made. Everywhere I look, I see something I never noticed before. Everywhere. God-damned clutter, like old bureau drawers. That's what I hate about this place. You can't move without running into something, it's so full of junk. I think she even made this table and the little rug in front of the fireplace, and those pillows. Cluttered house of junk. I can't stand it.

No.

That's not what's really bothering you. Who are you kidding? You've lived in junky places, dirty places.

This place is clean, the cleanest I ever lived in. And all the stuff all over. It's all good. Pretty. Good for people. Sally makes something beautiful out of everything. Even the damned soap dish in my bathroom is a shell from some beach in Oregon.

Why do I resent it so much?

I didn't resent the Meyer's house. Money. Simple as that. The difference between them and me is money. Money to buy the best house, the best furniture, the best paintings, the best dishes, the best

109

food. That just told me what I always knew. The difference between me and the ones who had it was money. Even their education. If I had money I'd have what they've got. Only more.

But this place isn't money. Sally wears those shabby skirts even my mother wouldn't look at. Everything here is something she made out of nothing. Take away all this stuff Sally makes, and you've got a wreck, a slum falling down the side of a hill. All this came out of Sally, like a spider spinning a web out of herself.

And she thinks I'm like her. She said it in the letters. We're some kind of soul-mates. Maybe I said it too. Well, I'm not like her. I couldn't do any of these things. I've tried. Everything comes out lousy.

I feel like nothing here. I feel like a bug in the corner someone forgot to sweep out.

The front door. It's her. She sees me, the wine bottle, tries to pretend she doesn't care. "Oh, you're home already, did you finish at Barbara's?"

"I only worked a few hours. She's got to get a debris box before I can go on. I go back Thursday. She gave me a tape recorder to help me write. I can dictate a poem, then listen."

"That's nice. Anything else new?" I don't answer. It was one of those dumb questions to fill space. She goes into the kitchen with a bag of groceries. I pour myself another glass of wine, and when I raise it to my mouth, I look up and see her in the doorway, watching me. Of course, she's frowning about the wine, but then the frown goes away, and she's looking at me deeper, deeper, as if she's trying to see something that's covered up, or at least to guess what's covered up. I want to yell at her, There's nothing! Understand that? If you get underneath the cover, you won't find anything!

"Have you called your mother since you got out?"

I wasn't expecting that. She's looking at me, puzzled. I shake my head and get up. Yossarian stands stiff in front of her. I turn and go down to my room before she can ask any more questions.

* * *

THIRD TIME AROUND. There is someone pulling out finally. How can the co-op increase sales and get out of the red if no one can find a parking place? Maybe, as Gary says, it's just a supermarket like any other one. I was so silly and defensive when he said that. He can't

110

understand my emotional involvement. He's probably right, I shouldn't keep seeing it as it was when we started, taking turns putting food on the shelves. Now it's a huge business. Lucky I just took him with me to buy groceries and not to one of those awful board meetings. So many things I do, seen through Gary's eyes, are empty middle-muddle activities.

Like those bumper strips. New ones plastered over the old ones, tattered, shredded, faded layers of remnants from old campaigns. Life is a bunch of old bumper strips. Stop giggling and concentrate on getting the rusty tailgate open. Drag out the cardtable and chair. Which box of leaflets?

Oh, God, isn't that funny. I forget why I'm manning the table today. It's not Sickle Cell Anemia, that was last week, the election is over and Sherry's doing the Women for Peace over at the El Cerrito Co-op. The kids have taken over the street Food Project collections and . . . of course, it's Save the Bay. What would Gary say if he saw me trying to remember why I'm here? Why should I care what he would say?

I drag table and chair and leaflets through the parking lot to the south door. More people come out that way. Coming out they're more likely to stop and chat, pick up a leaflet. Also, the free-kittens kids, Panthers and knife-sharpener tend to stay up near the phone booths. Less crowded here. Colder draft though. My legs should be permanently blue from sitting in drafts like this.

Lay out piles of leaflets, each held down by a rock from that excavation near Live Oak Park; there, the striped red one in the middle, as usual, something bright and warm to look at when I feel cold. Too bad Yossarian can't come and sit on my feet, keep me warm. But too many dogs run loose around here. There are more dogs than people now in Berkeley, I think.

"Hi, Carmen! Boyd." She's cut her hair, nice.

"Ruby. I'm Saving The Bay today. Ruby nods and signals that she has the literature. Here's a new face. He'll take a leaflet. But he doesn't look at me. That means he's only being polite, he'll throw it away. Don't be polite and waste paper! There are the Steadmans. I thought she was sick. The young ones pass by, looking through or over me. Times have changed. Before, the young ones always stopped, talked, helped. Now they hurry past, buy their brown rice and French wine, then go home again.

"Hi, Sally."

"Judy. But you're early." She leans against the edge of the card table. She's so small and light, it hardly wiggles. "You're not taking over till twelve—or did I get the schedule wrong?"

She shakes her head.

"It wouldn't surprise me. You know, I was getting out of the car and I couldn't remember what table I was manning? I'm going senile, I think."

She laughs. Such a tiny woman, with such a large mouth when she laughs. Most people keep their lips tight when they laugh, but Judy lets go and opens her mouth wide, a big, deep laugh. "No, you're all right. I have some shopping to do, so I thought I'd come early, take care of that, then take over the table. How's business?"

I shrug. "I just started, but it'll be as usual. They stop to visit, but no one wants to take a leaflet. They say they already know, and besides it's just a waste of paper. Petitions are still good, people stop to sign, but . . ."

Judy nods, still laughing. "I caught an awful cold last time." Then she stops laughing and shifts her eyes away from mine. "Also I came a little early to talk to you about something."

I'm handing a leaflet to old Olaf, who usually reads them and analyzes them with me. This time he just takes it silently and goes into the store. I turn back to Judy to hear what she has to say.

She hesitates. "You know . . . Gary came to work for us."

I nod and feel apprehension creeping up my legs, like the cold draft.

"Did he say anything to you?"

I shake my head.

"By the time he got there it was almost lunch time. Jake showed him the back yard. Said he could start with the dead tree, and, depending on how long it took to dig it out, he might go on to some weeding and pruning. Then Jake left. I gave Gary lunch. Then I had to go show a house."

She hesitates and I wait.

"When I got back . . . well, you see, I forgot to mention I'd offered him a glass of wine at lunch . . ."

I almost don't have to listen to the rest.

". . . he'd taken the jug down into the garden. He was sort of leaning on the shovel when I came back about two hours later. The jug was almost empty, the tree hardly touched. He started digging, but I think he was too stoned to do much. And it was sunny, you

112

know. He started sweating and got awfully flushed. I was afraid he was going to be sick. I went back into the house. Every once in a while I'd look out the window. Sometimes he'd be sitting there drinking the wine. Then he'd dig a little. Then he got the axe and sort of hacked at it. Well, by the time Jake got home, he'd made an awful mess, but the tree was still there. Jake pitched in with him and they got it out finally, and he left. He sort of lurched out, looking sullen and angry . . . and awfully drunk. Jake was furious. He blamed me, of course, for giving him wine, and we had a awful row. But how was I to know . . . you didn't mention he had a drinking problem."

I need a long sigh before I answer her. "I didn't know. But you're right, there's a drinking problem and I don't know how to handle it, what to do. He doesn't touch hard liquor, but he's gone through all our wine. I'm sorry, I had no idea he would do that on the job."

"Well, Jake was furious with me at first. But finally he cooled off. We're in one of our good phases now. We talked about it, wondered if we should call you and tell you. Jake said no. Then we thought, next time he comes to work we should just tell him, no booze. But I don't want to . . . to offend him."

"Well, you're the ones who've been offended."

"Yes, in any other case we just wouldn't hire the man again. We had a man once who did that the we just laughed about it and never hired him again. But this is different . . . This . . ."

"Certainly no one expects you to put up with this for my sake." I'm so angry I could just shake Gary. Why did he do it?

"It's not just for your sake." Judy shakes her head and gives an embarassed smile. "You know, it's funny, but somehow I feel as if *I'm* in the wrong."

"You?"

"Not just me. Us. All of us. I was standing there watching him from the window, unable to just go down there and say, look, we're not paying you to guzzle our wine! I mean, I felt he was daring me to say something, and that if I did, it would prove some awful thing about me, expose some terrible truth. He . . . he makes me feel so guilty."

I nod.

"You too? How could you? After what you did for him . . ."

I shrug. "I didn't do anything. Nothing compared to . . ."

Judy's hands are fluttering now, as they always do when she's excited. "It's what he's been through, I guess. It's given him some moral position, so far above us, so high, that he's not subject to the same rules, or . . .''

"That's nonsense! I'm going to have to speak to him, that's all.''

My voice sounds very clear and certain, but I don't feel that way inside. I can imagine the look on his face when I tell him there have been complaints about his drinking. Maybe Bob would do it for me. Man to man, easy on the booze, friend. No. Bob did all he's going to do when he let me invite Gary. Now Gary is my problem. Bob won't notice anything he does, if he can help it.

"And, for heaven's sake, don't tell Jake I told you. He said we've either got to tell Gary ourselves or just not hire him. But I knew what would happen. One more incident, and Jake would just wash his hands of Gary. Bang. Final. Jake will do anything for a person, but he won't stand feeling used. Not for a minute. I do want Gary to have a chance. I want to help.'' Judy's eyes are filling.

I turn away from her, shoving leaflets at people as if stabbing them with knives. "No, I won't say anything to Jake.'' I keep shoving the leaflets at people. They look at my face and they take the leaflet as if they're afraid not to.

"Well, I'll do my shopping, then come back. Want me to bring you some coffee?''

I nod my head and she steps on the treadle that swings the big glass door wide, sweeping me with another cold draft of air rushing into the store. One day I'll freeze here, petrify with a scrap of useless paper in my hand. They'll find me with icicles dripping from my eyes, and they'll say of me, like the tiger in "Kilimanjaro'' that no one knows exactly what she was doing there.

* * *

SAM PUTS the hammer down, right at twelve o'clock. "Let's eat. Did you bring your lunch?'' First thing he's said all day except, "Hold this,'' or "Hand me that.''

I shake my head. "I'll go out and get something.'' I start down the hall, then turn around. "Want a beer?''

"No beer on the job,'' he snaps. "I've got plenty of food. You can share my lunch.''

I'm standing there, feeling myself go hot all over. He doesn't even look at me, just starts opening a paper bag. What gives this little fart the idea he can give me orders?

114

Then I'm sitting down on the floor and he's handing me an apple and half his cheese sandwich. He takes small, really dainty bites, cool and thoughtful. I'm sweating and panting and so hungry I'm stuffing the food down between deep breaths.

"Take you a while to get in shape," he says, and then looks off into space, cool and inhuman.

"You do a lot of sheet rock?" He nods. "Christ, what miserable work. Heavy damned stuff. Mud and tape and mud."

He nods. "Tedious. More fun to work with natural wood. But sheetrock's a nice material. Fireproof. Looks good and fresh when it's all done."

"You do much of this kind of work?"

"Most of the work is like this. Once in a while I get to build a nice cabinet or something, but this is the bread and butter." He hands me a bag of nuts and then he's quiet again.

"You did time." I say it as if to tell myself. I can't imagine this guy at The Farm.

He nods.

"How long?"

"Two years at the C.O. camp, two more in prison."

Longer than I did. I wait but he doesn't say any more. Sally and all her friends talk all the time, except this one. "I guess you just want to forget all about it."

Now he looks at me. "Oh, no. I don't think a person should forget anything so important. That was probably the most important period of my life."

"Me too," I say, and then we're both quiet again. I've really been waiting to talk to this guy, and it turns out he's the hardest one of all to talk to.

"Of course, my experience was different from yours." He knows I want to compare notes. "Half the time I was at the C.O. camp, only half at the federal prison, after I escaped."

"You escaped?"

He shrugs and smiles. "It was called that. I walked away. It was a sort of ritual some of us did, an added protest to the war, to remind them we were still here, still opposed. What we did was just walk away, then go to a city and notify the FBI and arrange for them to pick us up."

"I guess they got rough."

He sort of laughs. "No, I'd say exasperated—fatherly. One of them kept saying, 'Look kid, just go back to the camp, you'll wreck your life with a real prison record, you'll never get a decent job, you're young, you'll wreck your life.' "

"But you didn't go back."

He shakes his head.

"How was the federal prison? Rougher than the camp."

He nods.

I have to question him to get anything but that nod. Every question I ask, he answers in that quiet way of his, but sometimes it's only yes or no. Just as much as I want to get from him I can have, but I have to ask for it.

"Pretty rough guys?"

"Yes."

"Ever give you a bad time?"

"Yes. To them I was a traitor, you see."

"What'd they do?"

"Came after me once."

"Hurt you?"

"I was in the hospital for a while."

"What happened to them?"

"Nothing."

"You didn't tell who did it?"

"No."

"And what'd they do after you went back?"

"Nothing. They left me alone after that."

"Weren't you afraid?"

"Yes, a little."

"But you don't sound bitter."

"They didn't understand. I think some of them were sorry."

We go on like this, question and answer, interrogation, like he doesn't want to say anything bad about these guys, like I'm asking the wrong questions and he'll answer politely but he won't open up until I ask the right ones. Then all at once he looks at his pocket watch and gets up, hammer in his hand.

So here I am standing in the middle of the floor again holding this fucking slab of sheetrock against the ceiling while he nails it up. He's running up and down a ladder, like a mouse running around me, moving fast so I can let go soon, never saying a word except that he's lucky I'm so tall. And I look at him and think no one would guess he had done time, harder time than I did. Nobody talking to him, even the kid-rapers must have thought they were too good for him. No library, no classes, no work. Restricted mail, all censored, rules against writing about the prison, about anything political, about anything . . . "Did you ever regret it? getting yourself put away? You could have got out of the draft maybe some other way."

He doesn't answer me. I stand there, holding up the damned ceiling, and he's just hopping around me like I didn't say a word. When he works, he works, and when he talks, he talks. Okay. Okay.

I hold sheetrock, I cut it, split little patches for here and there. Measure, cut. Nail up. Hit my finger! Same finger again. Jesus Christ, again. "Fuck!"

"That always happens when you start getting tired. Let's take a break."

He pulls out his watch and I'm surprised to see it's three o'clock. Pours tea from his thermos bottle and hands me the cup.

"Sometimes I regretted it," he says, like I asked the question just now instead of an hour ago. "When I was very low. But not for long. I was very idealistic, and there were some people who believed in me. That's why it was so much easier for me than for you. I had made a choice."

"You really made a choice? You knew what you were doing? And what would happen if you did it?"

"Yes, I think so."

"I can't believe that." I look at him to see if he's taking offense, but he just has that same cool, listening look. "Everyone says they choose one thing or another, but I never really see them doing it, just telling later how they chose it. And how can you really think you chose something if you hadn't already been in it, experienced it, known where you were headed?"

He nods. "Of course, you're right. I just meant that I did consciously make a choice, knowing something of the consequences."

"When? I mean, exactly at what minute did you decide you were not going to fight?"

He laughs. "I always call it the moment when I decided *to* fight . . . to resist, to hold my ground against the draft, against the way everyone was being caught up in the killing without really knowing why, without making a true decision."

He's playing with words. Or is he putting off telling me, stalling for time to think of a good story? No, not him.

"I was out walking. I used to walk a lot, out in the country. You could do that then. I'd take an apple and a canteen of water and go out all day. Ever do that?''

I shake my head. Next he'll be telling me about his boy scout medals.

''I was walking. And I came to a huge park, and then to a military cemetery. You know how they look. All those little white crosses in absolutely straight lines, going up over the hill, and down the other side, where I couldn't see them, but I knew how they would go, still in straight lines. And I thought, there they are, still at attention, still lined up, taking orders, even in death. And that was when I knew I wasn't going, no matter what they did to me.''

I nod at him. ''That's how I feel. That's exactly how I feel.''

''Is it.'' His face is blank. Maybe he doesn't believe me, doesn't see me in his class, no, I'm in a class with the convicts who put him in the hospital.

''I got to know a political at The Farm,'' I tell him. ''That's how I got started reading.''

''Good. I like to think we did some good in there.''

''You didn't think so.''

''It didn't show when I was there.''

''Did you ever get friendly with any regular guys?''

He nodded. ''Couple of murderers. Got drunk and killed someone, couldn't even remember doing it. Simple men. Kind.''

Then he's up again, swinging that hammer like it's only nine o'clock in the morning, humming to himself. I'm dragging and I start slowing down. A couple of times he waits, then he says, ''Hurry up.'' Then the next few times, he waits before telling me to hurry up again. I look at his face. It's smooth and fresh and relaxed. He's not getting mad at me for dragging, and I find that if I push myself, even though I'm really tired, I feel better than if I just drag along. So he's always right.

Maybe that's why I don't like him. Or maybe it's because of the way he can look back on the time he did . . . like it was a choice, even an honor. Because he was so sure. Total conviction. In his own way, this little guy is the cockiest, more sure, secure guy I've ever seen. No wonder both women he married left him.

''Jesus, work like this is harder than doing time!''

He laughs. ''You get used to it.''

Not me.

* * *

"GARY, YOU'VE GOT to do something about the drinking!" It's out. Not the way I planned. I was going to wait for the right moment, bring it up in a kindly way, a casual way. As if I ever could make a plan my feelings would follow. Wrong time, wrong place. he stands stooped, rigid, as if frozen with his hand in the cabinet.

"It's my own bottle."

"I know. Because I stopped buying wine. That's absurd, for us to stop buying wine because you drink too much."

Silence. Then, "Don't you think that's my problem?"

"No, it's mine too, if you drink all our wine, then buy your own, so you're half-stoned all the time and too drunk to work!" Oh, my God, I didn't mean to add that.

"Who says I'm too drunk to work?"

Now I'm silent, then a deep breath. Oh, what's the use. "The Meyers, Judy told me."

"They complained about me drinking?" He is drawn up to his full height now, mortally offended.

"Yes."

"They offered me wine and then complained about my drinking."

"They offered you wine at lunch. They didn't tell you to take the bottle into the garden with you."

"Oh, I see you have all the details. You must have had a nice talk about me. When was this?"

"Saturday."

"I see. A full report on the behavior of the felon. And what did your friend Sam add in his report?"

"Nothing. I mean, I haven't talked to Sam about you."

"Didn't he tell you I wanted to have a beer and he said no, and so I didn't? Simple. Easy. Your friends should have tried it. They could have told me. Why didn't they?"

I stand with my hands on the sink, hanging on, feeling I might drop from . . . some position, feeling wrong, wrong. "Yes, they could have, but . . . it shouldn't be necessary. I . . . yes, it was wrong to talk about you behind your back, but . . ." How is this happening? How am I being put on the defensive? "It's very hard to tell you anything, Gary. You're so hostile?"

"Hostile? What have I done that's hostile?"

119

"It's the way you look. Angry. Chronically angry. You make people feel as if they've done you some terrible injury."

"Maybe that's how I feel, maybe you'd feel that way too if . . ."

"You can't go on feeling that way forever."

"How long can I? What's my time limit? Give me a schedule."

I dry my hands and keep them wrapped in the towel. "I don't understand you, Gary. I don't know you at all. I thought from your letters . . . I got an entirely different impression."

"So did I."

"What do you mean?"

"Nothing. What else? Go on, what else do you want to say to me?"

Shall I? It's too late to back up now. "I thought you cared about reading, writing. I haven't seen you pick up a book. Have you done any writing?"

"No."

"In the two weeks you've been here you haven't done anything but drink and sleep and . . . tell horror stories at the dinner table. Bob . . ."

"Oh, he's complained about me too."

"I think he's right. At first I didn't, but every night there's an assault on us. He said it, if it's not a lecture on eating meat it's some sickening story about the prison. That's what I mean by hostility. Gary, sometimes I think you act as if you're still in prison, that you don't see where you really are, don't see us as . . ."

"Sometimes I feel this place is a prison!"

"I don't understand."

"You wouldn't. You're used to it."

How does he do that? He makes me feel that there is something terrible here, something bad that only he can see. "We're not perfect, I'm sure, but by comparison . . ."

"With where I might end up, with where I belong, with where I'd be if you hadn't pulled me out . . ."

"My God, Gary, do you resent me for helping you? Because if that's true, I don't see how . . ."

"I don't resent you for helping me. I just resent being treated like a half-crazy lush who might . . ."

"Well, if you act that way, what do you expect!" Oh, how stupid. Big breath. "Look, I don't mean that, I . . ."

120

But he's not there when I turn to look at him again. I hear him thumping down the stairs. Then he's coming up again. I go to the door of the living room and see he has his coat on. "Gary . . ." He stalks across the living room to the front door, jerks it open and slams it behind him.

Mother and Yossarian are sitting side by side on the sofa.

Yossarian barks, twice.

Mother says, "Good riddance."

But I am thinking about the expression on his face as he pulled open the door. It was exactly the look of satisfaction that I see on Mother's face. Satisfied, vindicated, even glad.

And I feel . . . how do I feel? As if I'd been handed a role to play, and I'd read my lines just the way he wanted me to.

* * *

CHRIST, MY HEAD. Who's screaming?

"You awake? Hey, Gary, wake up, move over, I have to get the baby's milk out of the refrigerator."

I open one eye and see table legs, then up, up, I see Margie. I'm stretched out on her kitchen floor, a pillow under my head and a sour, moldy-smelling blanket over me.

"Just like old times," Margie says and laughs. "You haven't changed."

I have, but she wouldn't understand. "Neither have you. You were pregnant when I left. You're still pregnant." She looks like she's just about to have it. There's the screaming again. It's the kid.

She pats her belly and frowns. "After this one, I'm going to tell that doctor to tie my tubes. Joe's against it, but he doesn't have the kids. I can't take the pills because of my blood pressure and nothing else works, nothing . . ." She goes into a long speech about all the ways she tries not to have kids. She looks a lot older. There's already gray in her hair. She's skinny except for the belly, dark circles under her eyes. To me it looks like it can't matter anymore how many kids she has. She looks finished. She looks older than Sally. Christ, she looks older than Sally's mother. In her eyes.

"What time did I get here?"

"Two o'clock. That's a.m.? Banging on the door. I thought it was Joe."

"Sorry."

"I was up with one of the kids anyway. I was sure surprised to see you. I didn't even know you were out."

I get up and sit at the table. It's full of dishes with food stuck on them, kid's toys, yesterday's newspaper. "Where's Joe?"

Her lips tighten and make a lot of new lines around her mouth. "He went looking for work. Three days ago. Someone told him there was something doing in Sacramento."

"Way up there? Why, can't he find work here?"

"He got fired again."

"Fight?" She nods and makes more lines around her mouth. Joe's a good laborer, strong, a hard worker, but he doesn't last on a job long, not with that temper. I look closer and see one of the circles under her eyes is darker than the other. Better change the subject. "You know, I came over here yesterday to look up all my old friends. I can't find anyone. You and Joe are the only ones. I went to Tommy's Bar. There isn't a Tommy's Bar anymore!"

She nods. "They took it out for the BART trains."

"God, was that a funny feeling!" I try to tell her what it was like, riding the bus down Mission Street, getting off on 24th, looking . . . that sudden lost feeling, like a bad dream. But she's busy with the kids, getting them to the table, feeding the little one on her lap. She keeps nodding, but I can't tell if she really hears me. Her attention is everywhere else, like parts of her spinning here and there, bouncing off me and the kids, and probably most of her worrying about Joe. I see a black spot on the table. It moves. My stomach heaves. Since when did I get so squeamish? I look around the room. It's bare, empty. No, that not true. It's full of crap, there's junk all over. But it's junk; garbage, stuff she set down and just forgot. Nothing homey. Like one of those burnt-out campfires at the beach, where there's nothing but beer cans and potato chip bags to show people were there.

"Where do the guys hang out now?"

She shrugs. "When Tommy's closed we stopped going out much. Couldn't afford it anyway, and that's no place to take kids. Joe sometimes goes out alone, but I don't know where." Her mouth gets tight again.

"Don't you ever hear from any of them? What about Steve?"

"Steve?" She looks confused. The baby is crying again, and the older one sits there looking at me and saying, Mommy, Mommy,

Mommy, like a chant. Margie shakes the baby up and down and it stops crying.

"Steve!" I say, laughing. "You know, with the bells on his motorcycle boots. We had a lot of laughs, remember?"

She looks at me with wide eyes. "You didn't hear?" She looks down again at the baby. "Steve was killed. Truck stopped short in front of him. He plowed into it and fell on his head. You know, he never would wear a helmet."

I'm quiet for a minute. "What about Johnny Mack? Did he marry that girl?"

She nods without looking at me. "Last I heard they were both in the hospital. Smack."

I go through the names. It's like a casualty list. Either they've dropped out of sight or are put away somewhere or they're dead. I save Penny for last. "I went to her place, but she moved."

"She didn't write to you?"

"A few times, then she stopped writing."

"She got married."

My voice is casual. "Anyone I know?"

She shakes her head and I know she's not going to tell me who Penny married or where she is. "She's happy."

"Good. Fine. I'm glad somebody is happy. I'm glad somebody is alive! I'm gone two years and I come back and find everyone wiped out."

"It's true." Then all of a sudden I see she's crying. Tears in wide streams down her face. "If you came here a few weeks from now, you wouldn't find us. Landlord sold the place. The new owner wants to paint it and triple the rent, get rid of the 'trash,' that's what he called us. We were always saying how we were going to get out of this dump. We're getting out all right. Jesus, where can we go?" The tears just keep running down her face. Eyes and nose all red. "You were all so smart. So fucking smart. And where are you all now? Dead."

"Hey, there's still you and Joe, you're all right."

"Until he picks a fight with the wrong guy and comes home minus an eye instead of just minus a job. When you came pounding on the door last night, I knew it wasn't Joe, I thought it was the police, come to tell me he was dead or locked up or something. All right, are we? Look at me, Christ, I'm only twenty-three years old and I'm an old woman."

Then she suddenly stops crying. It's all over. Margie was always like that. Tears still in her eyes, but she was through crying, smiling. That was when she looked the prettiest. She almost looks pretty again now. "But you look good, Gary. Where are you staying?"

"In Berkeley. There's this woman I started writing to . . ."

"Ahh . . ."

"No, not like that. She's fifty, married, family. Has a house on the hill. Her husband's a teacher. She got me paroled. I live with them now."

"Gee!" She leans forward, bright and alert, like the old Margie, the way she looked when she sat on the back of Joe's bike, hands set on her thighs, erect and ready to go. "That's wonderful."

"I write. I'm a writer."

She frowns. "What do you write?"

"Mostly poetry."

"Poetry? You?" She giggles.

"I've already been published. And there's this teacher at Bay College over there says I have talent."

Now she's really impressed. "A published writer. Who would have thought . . . you'll be rich and famous and I'll be able to say I knew you. I always thought Joe should be an artist of some kind. That's why he gets mad, loses his temper, he's so passionate, and he really used to draw good, remember? Maybe he ought to try again. There's a lot of money in it. He could illustrate your books . . ."

I let her go on talking. I don't tell her that I'm not making any money writing, or that I left Sally's house. I tell her Joe's a great artist. I tell her about Sally's house, all the beautiful stuff in it, and all the meetings there, and the influential friends Sally has. I tell her as soon as Joe turns up, we'll start on a book together. I tell her what she wants to hear.

And while I'm telling her, without thinking, without having to make any effort to sound real or credible, just pouring it all out like reciting the Gettysburg Address in the fifth grade, I remember how I did this before, here, or at Tommy's. I remember how we all talked about our contacts, our possibilities, our big plans. We were, none of us, going to end up simple working stiffs like our stupid parents or some of the dumb kids we went to school with. No, not us.

We weren't going to be dopers either, or convicts, or dead.

I watch her eyes brighten up and her back straighten. She can hardly wait for Joe to come back so she can tell him. Tell him what?

All these lies. Dreams. That's what we all lived on. Dreams. It's not like lying. She'll never call me on it, never expect me to follow through. She'll probably forget it an hour after I'm gone. She knows. But for a while, she's cheered up. That's all she'll ever have, a few dream jolts while she lives out this . . .

"Where you going?"

I realize I'm standing up. My legs are aching like I have to run, run, get away from here.

"I thought you were going to stay for Thanksgiving. Last night you said . . ."

"I forgot. My mother. I promised her I'd see her today. I better go. No, don't get up, I know my way out."

"You ought to."

"Goodbye, Margie."

"Hurry back. Maybe Joe'll be here. We'll make plans."

"Yeah."

I almost run down that long hall to the front door. I hold my breath. There's a smell in this place. A familiar smell I'd forgotten, leaky gas heaters turned on full blast, rotting food, baby piss and . . . big plans.

* * *

I LOOK at the turkey and feel as Gary might, if he were here. A corpse, stuffed and charred. A blood ceremony. Thanksgiving. Barbarians tearing the flesh off the bones with their teeth.

"Wonderful dinner, Sally," says Millie, small and demure beside Barbara, who laughs too loud.

"Thank you, Millie." Yes, share my flesh, my food, my husband. When he said she would be alone on Thanksgiving, I told him, without a thought, to invite her too. Generosity? Suicide? Contempt. I felt nothing but contempt for both of them when I said it. A certain curiosity about how low they could sink, how squalid. Maybe they play footsie under the table, my table. Maybe that's a necessary part of the thrill.

I'm the one who's being squalid. Self-pity. I couldn't be more sorry for myself. Depressed. Feeling such a failure. Can't seem to hide it. Everyone knows, and knows why. Not Bob and Millie. Gary. Judy keeps smiling at me anxiously, Jake addresses his remarks to me, as if I am the only one with intellect enough to understand them.

125

Barbara reaches out to pat me on the arm. Even John is respectful toward his father and his grandmother, for my sake. My wounds are so visible. Only Sam looks unaware, bleak, his usual silence deep and withdrawn. He misses his children desperately on holidays.

"Where's Gary?" says Dennis. "I guess he's spending Thanksgiving with his mother?" His dark face is inquiring, then confused as he sees the silence he has produced.

Finally I say, "I suppose he might be. I don't know."

Dennis waits, looks around. Sees faces staring into plates. "I take it . . . things haven't been going too well. Are we not to talk about it?" Deep, velvety voice. So soothing. No one can resist a question from that voice. I was determined not to talk about Gary when he wasn't here to defend himself, and my silence only made everyone uncomfortable. Dennis makes talking possible. Not a betrayal, no, a search.

"Tell me, Dennis, have you had any contact with him?"

Dennis looks disappointed, even hurt. "Not since that day he came to the college with John."

John looks up. "I dropped him in your office, then I never saw him again until I picked him up at four in the cafeteria."

Dennis nods. "We only shook hands and talked for a minute. I had a class coming up. I invited him to sit in on it. He came to class with me, sat in the back." Dennis's color deepens, a blush of embarrassment. "It wasn't one of my best days, I guess. After a few minutes, Gary got up and left."

"Very rude," mutters Mother, making a clicking, disapproving noise with her lips.

"No, ma'am, not really." Dennis nods respectfully toward Mother, and she blushes with pleasure in spite of herself. Then she pushes at her meat and frowns. Oh, dear, it's like last night. She can't coordinate knife and fork to cut it, and she'll be angry if I do it for her in front of everyone. I've got to get her to a doctor no matter how hard she fights it.

"He left a note at my office, said he was sorry but he just couldn't sit through a class. Something about his past experience in schools. A lot of people feel that way, associate the classroom with pain. Understandable. That's why, when the weather permits, I try to take my class out on the lawn, anywhere but a classroom."

Yet he was so eager to go to college. What did he think it was? "You haven't seen him since?" I ask.

"No. He said on the note he'd pick a better time to talk to me."

"But he hasn't."

Dennis touches the tip of his fork to his plate in short, soundless jabs. "I think that may be my fault. Often beginning writers are...so frightened about their work, so afraid of criticism, afraid even to bother someone by asking him to read it. After all, I'm only a couple of blocks away. I should have walked over one evening. I told him to drop in anytime, but he might have thought I was just being polite." Now Dennis looks guilty. If anyone is sensitive, it is Dennis, not those he makes excuses for. Still, maybe he does understand something about Gary that I don't. Maybe it has something to do with being creative.

"But," says Bob, "you told him his stuff was good, why should he be afraid?"

Dennis smiles. "You're direct, logical, assertive. Admirable qualities. Gary probably doesn't have them. Many people don't." I see Bob's old, incurable contempt for homosexuals still there in his look, and Dennis's patient, cool recognition of it as he looks back at Bob. "Artists are—difficult people. Not like the rest of us. Some of us... the best we can hope for is...to make ourselves agreeable. Artists are never agreeable." And now the deeper sadness comes into Dennis's eyes. He is, after all, regardless of his looks, not a boy. He must be nearly forty. He has given up writing. And his last roommate left six months ago. There are so many forms of loneliness, one deeper than another.

"Then," Bob leans forward, "you think he really is an artist?"

Dennis hesitates. "It depends on so many things. He could be. If he can make certain decisions. If conditions are right. Certainly there's talent, of course, there's talent."

Bob looks annoyed. The rest of us are silent, but understand Bob's annoyance. I have heard Dennis say these very words so many times. Talent, he sees talent everywhere.

Barbara breaks the silence. "What do you suppose he did all day, between the time he left your class and the time he met John?"

John looks up, his face severe, all his usual cool passivity dropped. "I can tell you where he was when I met him. In the gamblers' corner of the cafeteria. Where people hang out who aren't even enrolled in the college. They come on campus, hassle the girls, play cards in the cafeteria, probably rip off a lot of things. No one knows for sure. No one knows how to get rid of them. Last week there was a stabbing, over a poker pot, I heard. So now, there's a no-gambling rule. But they're afraid they might have to call the police to enforce it, and we'll have a riot.''

"You think he was there all day?''

"He looked to be on pretty intimate terms with them...yes, I'd say he'd been sitting there long enough to have gotten pretty well acquainted.''

"Birds of a feather,'' snaps Mother, and John can't help making a little, stiff motion like a nod.

So their late night camaraderie didn't last long. John looks the way he used to when I punished him for teasing his sister. He is jealous of the attention I've given Gary. That's why he grabbed this opportunity to...to inform on him. Oh, John, how silly, how ignoble, that the only feeling you show me for the past year should be this. John looks at me, drops his glance and puts on the mask of passivity again. Oh, John, is that all that's alive in you, my infant, envy and spite?

"I hope when he comes back,'' says Dennis, "you'll tell him I'll be glad to see more of his work.''

"He may not come back.''

"I think he will,'' says Jake. "You're forgetting the objective realities of the situation. According to the conditions of his parole, he has no alternative. He will come back here, or be returned to prison.'' Jake leans back in his chair and raises a finger, ready to go on with his analysis, but I don't let him.

"Maybe that's why he's not happy here,'' I say, and all of a sudden I spill over. "I don't know what it is. I'm so confused. He's like a different person. He doesn't read or write or...he looks at me as if I'm one of his prison guards...and maybe that's what happened... in being part of the provisions of his parole, I must seem to him to be...'' My burning throat closes up and my eyes overflow. How stupid. I didn't want this to happen. Not to embarass anyone. Not, even more, not to condemn Gary with my tears.

"What do you hear from Nancy?'' Sam says, in a clear, resolute voice. He gives me a look that says, no self-pity. "Any more pictures of that grandson?'' Thank you, Sam.

"Yes, I haven't shown you the ones that came last week. Nancy called this morning. Said to wish you all a Happy Thanksgiving. Her husband has got his grant renewed. From the Defense Department, of course. For what, I don't know. I don't want to know.''

128

* * *

"COLMAN RESIDENCE." Funny how her voice always trembles, like she's. . . not exactly afraid, but not expecting good news.

"Hi, Ma."

"Gary?"

"Sure. How are you?"

"You're out already?"

"That's right."

"Oh, that's good. I'm so glad. You're all right?"

"I'm fine. I been living in Berkeley, with those people I wrote you about."

"Really?" She says it like she never believed me. "That's nice." Her voice is fading, like she's drifting away.

"I'm sorry I couldn't get you yesterday, but I couldn't find the phone number. It was stuck way inside my wallet. We could have had Thanksgiving together."

"Oh, well, I had to work anyway, serve a big dinner." I wait, but that's all she says.

"Don't you want to see me, Ma?"

"Of course, yes, Dear. I'll be through early today, about two."

"What's the address?"

"I'll meet you. There's a coffee shop out on. . ."

"Tell me where you are. All I've got is this phone number and a post office box."

"Yes. Well, I don't have any place here to see visitors, but we could meet and have a nice. . ."

"Well, you could tell me where you are, for Christ's sake!" She doesn't answer. "You said Colman. All I have to do is look up the name in the phone book."

"They're unlisted." It's a shaky whisper, that little choked up sound before she starts crying.

"All right, if you don't want to see me. . ."

"I do, I do, Gary, but I don't want you to come here, not just yet."

"All right, I promise I won't, but you can still give me your address."

"No, Gary. This is a good job. This is the last good job I'll have. These people treat me real good. I know you mean to do right, but sometimes you. . . you're not yourself." She clears her throat and

129

makes her voice steady. "I can't have you showing up here drunk in the middle of the night sometime and...."

"That was over two years ago. Christ, you haven't seen me for over two years! I've changed."

"I'm glad, Gary. That's what I prayed for."

"But you don't believe it."

I hear her take a breath. "Not just from you telling me, no. So many times you told me you changed, and I believed. Now, if you have, I'll know, little by little, I'll see you make a life for yourself. That's what I want you to do, make a good life for yourself. You're still young. I always believed you could. With your brains, your talent. Everyone always said it, Gary. Remember how those teachers used to talk about you? Even the police. Every time you got in trouble, they was always pulling out those intelligence tests and saying how high you scored."

"But you don't trust me."

"Gary?" Her voice is trembly again. "You said you was all fixed up with those people in Berkeley. Did something happen?"

"No, what could happen?"

"I just thought maybe...sometimes you have such high hopes, you exaggerate...or, you didn't do something to...."

"What do you mean, exaggerate? They're fine people, upper class. You should see their house, up on the hill, a view clear across The Bay. I can probably stand at the window and see where you are. I have my own room. They got me a couple of jobs, gardening, stuff like that. But I'm going to get something better. They have a lot of influential friends. One of them is a college professor. He says I'm talented. I'm going to be a writer."

"That's fine, Dear."

"You don't believe a word I'm saying. You think I'm drunk and just talking. I haven't had a drink in two years, and I...."

"No, I believe you, Dear. They sound like fine people. You have a chance for a whole new life. Gary, try to make the most of it, this time, don't...."

"Okay, okay! I didn't call you up for a lecture."

She doesn't say anything. I can hear her breathing. "Gary." Her voice breaks, and I feel this awful pain in my throat, like a knife cutting. I swallow hard. "Gary, I'm still your mother. If you need help, just tell me."

130

"I don't need help. I'm fine. I just thought you might want to see your son."

"I do, Dear, I do. At the Cottage Coffee Shop. Corner of Polk and . . ."

I hang up.

* * *

SURELY I CAN FINISH knitting the cap in time to send it to Nancy for Christmas. Maybe even some matching mittens. It'll take longer than the baby's cap. I hope she likes it. However she has changed, she still skis. There is no way we could disagree politically on skiing. Ecologically? Oh, don't think about it.

How quiet the house is. I don't think I've been alone in the house for . . . I can't remember. It was good of Bob to take Mother to the doctor. And Women for Peace cancelled the meeting. Unbelievable, a stretch of time, two hours or more, alone and quiet. I wonder if monks or nuns knit. No, they learn how to sit still, doing nothing but thinking about God. I could never do that. I have to do something. Of course, they're *doing* something, but . . .

Oh, no. Yossarian, who is it? Maybe if we don't answer the door, whoever it is will go away. When they ring the bell, we'll just pretend . . . key in the lock, door opening. It must be John.

No.

Gary. Paler than ever. Unshaven. Hair limp and oily, clothes wrinkled. He coughs. He's caught a cold. But he looks at me steadily. At least he's not drunk. Surprising that Yossarian hasn't leaped at him. Not wagging his tail either, but still, listening, not so hostile.

"Hello, Gary."

"Hi." His voice is eager. He even gives a little nod. Is he hoping I'm not angry? Of course, I'm not . . . want to pretend nothing happened? Yes, that's the best way. I see his legs above my knitting. He moves to stand near the fire.

"I went to San Francisco."

"Oh, good. Did you see your mother?"

"No. She was too busy. She . . . she won't let me come to where she works. Afraid I'll disgrace her. Did I ever tell you that? She would never even give me the address to write to. Afraid some day her bad penny would turn up."

I don't answer. He wants pity for being rejected by his mother. I do. I pity him. I pity her too.

"I guess I don't blame her," he says.

I keep knitting because I don't know what else to do. But I can't leave him alone in his misery. He has reached out. I must meet him now. I raise my eyes and look into his. His eyes are clear but too wide, frightened. "They're all dead over there," he says. He moves toward me, sits down on the chair opposite me. Yossarian gets up and goes to sit near the fire. "The place where we used to hang out is gone. Gone. The whole building. I finally found one old friend. Everyone I asked her about...they're dead or in prison. Wiped out. Like a bomb fell on them. Nothing left. And it was only a couple of years ago. Lives just...wiped out. Except a few. A girl I used to go with. She got married. She doesn't want me to know where she is either." For a second he gives me his little crooked smile. "But the worst was when this friend, Margie, do you remember I wrote to you about her?" I nod. "...when she started talking about the future. Just the way we used to. We all had big plans, big. So big, there wasn't anything small we could do to get there. Great future. Then I looked at her and I could see, she has no future."

He stands up again and goes to the fireplace. He is shivering and coughing. Yossarian comes back to sit by me. "I started walking. I walked downtown and went to a movie, where I could get warm. I fell asleep. They kicked me out at midnight and I walked for the rest of the night. All the way to the beach, up and down on the sand until daylight. I had breakfast in one of those joints at Playland. That's being torn down too.

"I went up by the Cliff House, but I looked so bad by then I didn't go in. I started walking again, following water. All up past Seacliff and over to the Marina. I hardly ever saw that side of town before. Then I ate again, went to another movie, slept there. I had money to eat, but not enough to stay in a hotel. At midnight I was out walking again, Fisherman's Wharf, North Beach. Plenty of people there, lights, all that strip stuff. I watched the pickpockets. Then I went down to Chinatown, found an all-night place where I kept ordering soup and coffee till the sun came up.

"Then I walked downtown and called my mother. I got mad when she wouldn't give me her address. She was right. I was yelling at her because she wouldn't trust me, and I was lying to her at the same time. Christ.

"It was sunny in the civic center. I sat there in the sun, with all the old winos. Then I went in the library, stayed there till it closed. Then another movie, with a midnight show. I was able to sleep there till three. I woke up with this cold, walked over to the freeway approach. A guy gave me a ride to Oakland."

My legs are aching from imagining him walking. I suppose he would have walked across the bridge if they had let him. "And you walked here from Oakland?"

He nods. "Sat in the sun, up the hill, on that big rock, until I knew everyone was gone but you. So you could tell me if you . . . if you still could . . ."

"Gary, if you're asking . . . I never told you to leave. It was you."

"I know."

"Maybe, since you've had time to think, you'll be able to tell me why you felt you had to leave . . . what went wrong, so that we can get along better."

"I don't know. I . . . writing to you was one thing. But . . . I was scared, I guess."

I laugh. I can't help it. "Scared? Of what?"

"You, This house. The way you live."

"I don't understand."

He sneezes. I point to the kleenex box. He takes a long time blowing. He trembles slightly. Feverish, scruffy, woebegone. This is no time for a heart-to-heart talk.

"Oh, for heaven's sake, it's so much simpler than we're making it. You've gone from one place to another that's just . . . just light-years away. Among strangers. Even I am a stranger. It's a shock. A terrible shock. Why don't we just leave it at that, and you go downstairs and go to bed before that cold turns into pneumonia."

He nods gratefully. "I need a hot shower."

"You certainly do."

"I'm not going to drink anymore."

"Good." I pick up my knitting again. "Dennis was asking about you. He said to drop in at his house any evening."

"Yes, I was going to do that. Yes, I'll do that." Silence. Now he'll go off and get cleaned up, sleep off his cold. Everything will work out. "How can you do that?"

I look up. "Do what? He is watching my hands. "Knit?"

"It's one stitch at a time, isn't it? I mean, the whole thing, when you finish it, is made of of a million loops, twisted through one another, one by one by one. How can you do it?''

"It keeps my hands busy."

He shakes his head. "I couldn't stand it."

I laugh. "It's like life. A stitch at a time, one little thing after another, finally making up a big pattern."

He keeps shaking his head. "Not my life. No." Then he stops shaking his head and looks at me as if he has just discovered something. "That's the difference between us." Then comes another coughing fit.

"You'd better get into that hot shower."

He nods, still coughing as he leaves the room.

I sit knitting and thinking about what he has said. He couldn't stand it. But he did. He made that purse out of cigarette packages, one at a time, as tedious as knitting, when he was in prison. But I guess he only did it because he was locked up and couldn't do anything else.

The phone rings. "Move, Yossarian." Oh, dropped some stitches! See to them later. Maybe not answer it? I'm coming, I'm coming. Probably too late. Keeps ringing. "Hello?"

"Sally."

Something wrong. I can tell the way Bob's voice sounds, that funny, evasive edge to it. "What's wrong?"

"I'm at the hospital. Your mother collapsed at the doctor's office. They've got her in intensive care."

"Which hospital?"

"No point in coming. They won't let you see her today. Do you want me to stay here for a while?"

"No. No, come home."

"I'm coming, Sally. I'm coming right home."

* * *

"I'M GLAD you came." We sit in the big leather chairs facing the fire and raise our glasses, big brandy glasses.

"I didn't know you lived so close to Sally," I answer. I don't tell him that I got lost a couple of times even though he's only two blocks away. The way these streets curve around, if you make one wrong turn, it takes you half an hour to get back. I don't think I'll ever get used to these curved, empty streets, no sound but the dogs barking at you when you go past a house. "Besides, I didn't want to bother you at home. I thought you'd want to see me at the college. I hope you didn't think, when I left your class..."

Dennis is shaking his head. "Classroom is no place for a serious writer. Maybe it's very healthy, your reaction."

"I thought I'd want to go there when I got out. You know, go-to-college, those were the magic words where I came from. Until I started writing to Sally I never knew anyone who went to college, except a couple of embezzlers, who were too good to talk to me. I don't know what I expected. But...it was just another school...rows of chairs."

"That's all it is." Dennis sighs. "Another school."

"Everyone seems so...young."

"We have lots of older students, much older than you."

"Sure, but I mean...innocent, naive." I don't know if I pronounced it right, but Dennis is just nodding, with no sign I said it wrong.

Dennis's house is different from Sally's or Barbara's or the Meyers'. Neat and small, lots of dark wood and thick carpets. And books, but his books are mostly hardbound, and not spread all over the place. Bookshelves everywhere, but organized and labeled. That wall's all poetry. This is the kind of house I would have. Comfortable. Masculine. The most masculine house I've ever seen, and it's owned by a queer.

"I think Sally's disappointed that I'm not going to the college."

"Did she say so?" He's fooling around lighting his pipe. He must have twenty of them on that rack. I think I'll get a pipe.

I shake my head.

Dennis looks at me, puffing big clouds of smoke around his dark face. Smoke and black leather and brown skin and dark turtle neck sweater. He's lost in a warm, dark shadow. I can hardly see him. "Why should she be disappointed?" Voice comes out of the cloud, deep and sweet as syrup. One thing I always did envy black guys was their voice.

"I think she expected someone different. I saw this old movie once where Joel McCrea gets locked up. He's innocent, of course, and when he gets out he goes to college, becomes a lawyer, marries a rich girl and saves innocent men from prison."

"Sally's not that simple-minded." Another puff of smoke. "Her son is your age, and he's no Joel McCrea."

"Maybe that's why she wishes I would be." I wait but he doesn't answer. He just waits for me to go on. "Well, I guess I'm afraid I'm not what she expected. I'm not even what I expected. You know something, the minute I heard my parole was granted, I went into a panic. First I was happy, but then I just panicked, and it was because I thought, now we'll be face to face, without time to compose, arrange things in a letter. Face to face. And I was scared shitless."

"Of not being what she expected."

"That's right." More, it seems I was scared of more, but I can't put my finger on that now.

He leans forward and pours more brandy into my glass. "And was she what you expected?" I nod my head and Dennis laughs. "You nod grimly, as if you wished she were not all you expected."

"She's running around all day and all night, working on ten different things. And she cooks and sews and paints and reads and plants things all over and plays the piano until sometimes I think. . . ."

He laughs. "Sally's a remarkable woman. Does she intimidate you?"

We sit for a few seconds and think about this. I hold my glass up, and Dennis's arm gestures toward the bottle. I help myself. I like the way he waits for a thought to digest, for another thought to grow, not limp and passive, really interested, really with me. "When I got out, I thought I wanted to forget everything. Wipe it out, my life, The Mission, The Farm, everything. I wrote that to Sally in one of my last letters. It was going to be like being born again." Dennis doesn't say anything. Nothing but smoke coming from that dark chair.

"When I was in, I tried to think of everything else but where I was. I started to read, to write, to do anything I could to forget it, to block it all out, to not live where I was, there, now, in the present. It's like I refused to live it, and so it all sat there waiting for me to live it through. Does that sound crazy?" He's not making a sound, not a move.

"So now it's with me all the time. Everything I see or hear reminds me of something there, by contrast, you know? I look at a plate of good food, and I think of the slop they served there, and I'm mad. It's alive in my mind, forcing me to live it.

"And not just The Farm. My whole life. I look at Sally, and I think what my mother is. I look at something in the house, and I remember the lack of it. The only thing that comes to my mind to say is what life

136

is like somewhere else, what it was back then. They don't want me always to be talking about that. So I have nothing to say. And then I start feeling...like...''

"Hostile? Angry?"

"That's right. The more they do for me, the more I'm so goddamned mad I can't see straight."

"You feel as if what you are, the experience that makes you what you are, is being rejected, is to be forgotten, wiped out. It must feel like an attack on you. Like someone wiping *you* out. It's healthy, I think, to hang on to everything you've experienced, to realize it must be a part of you, assimilated."

"Not if it makes me mess up my chances."

"It needn't."

"What do you mean?"

"You're a writer, aren't you?" He leans forward and I can see his face glistening like all that rich, polished wood. His eyes are bright. "That's where a writer has it all over everyone else. All the pain, the agony, every terrible thing you've been through. It's all grist for the mill. Of course, you shouldn't talk about it with Sally and her family. You must save it, store it up, hoard it, your treasure. It all goes into your writing." He sinks back into the chair, and the silence in the room is like after one of those preachers my mother used to take me to hear.

"You think I'm a writer," I say. "I mean, you really meant those things you said about my poems."

"Of course, I did."

"You think I'm talented."

"Everyone has some talent." That wasn't what I wanted to hear. He knows I'm waiting for more. "You have talent, of course, but it takes more than talent. You must have something to say..."

"I've got something to say, Christ knows."

"...and the drive, the intensity that keeps you at it. And the right conditions...no writer is going to develop among the workers on a banana plantation in Brazil."

"Yeah." I'm nodding my head, just leaning back and nodding. Is it possible he's right? I want him to be right. I want to believe that this thing grinding in me, and the fear and anger all mixed up together, and the way all the things that ever happened to me are filling me, filling me until I'm ready to bust, that they all come from something real, that they all mean I'm superior, they all . . . shit, that's the brandy talking. With half a heat on I can always believe that every mess I make is just a sign of my hidden genius.

"How much have you got done?"

"Done?"

"Since you came to Sally's. What have you been writing? I'd be glad to see more if you want me to . . ."

I shake my head. "I haven't done anything."

"Nothing? Not a line? Well, there you are!" He laughs, a deep, rich chuckle, like I proved his point, like I just explained everything. That's right, that's what I want to hear. We both lean forward now and agree that, of course, I've been coming apart because I need to be writing, and he quotes a line from one of my poems and jumps up, gets a book, and compares it to another poem, and I feel higher than the brandy could ever make me feel.

After another hour, I tell him, "Christ, I'm glad you understand. You're the only one I can talk to. You really understand." I'm feeling good, and it's not just the brandy.

"It's the only thing, the writing. Without it, life goes to pieces," he says.

"But you quit. You don't write anymore."

He shrugs. "I learned my limitations. Now I try to help others, who do write. That's something. I'm still part of it."

"Will you help me? Let me come and talk to you?"

"Sure. Anytime you want to."

"You're the only one I can talk to."

"I'm flattered."

I lean back and take one more sip of the brandy. Relaxed. Easy. It's true, I feel at ease with him. Maybe it's because he believes in me, calls me a writer and wants to help. Maybe it's because he believes I'm in some way superior to him because I'm writing and he's not. Maybe it's because he's queer, so no matter what he has or does or says, I still know I'm better than he is.

* * *

"YOU CAN SIT with her as long as you like. If she regains consciousness, don't be surprised if she doesn't know you."

The doctor is younger than I. All doctors seem to be younger than I. And bored. I can tell that Mother is going to die, because the

138

doctor is uninterested, eager to get away. And because I can visit with her as long as I like, not a word about being careful not to tire her.

The woman in the other bed looks angry. I nod at her, but she turns away. She knows Mother is dying too, and she resents her. I pull the curtains closed, all around the bed. I will hide Mother's shame, her dying, behind the curtains. Mother's manners were always so perfect. She would not want to offend anyone in her dying.

"Mother. It's Sally." Your hand is cold. No response, not even the quiver of an eyelid. You sleep deeply. For so long you complained of sleeping poorly. But now your sleep is heavy, so deep, as if you are sure to wake refreshed and alert.

I stand holding your hand as I used to at the street corner while we watched the light change and I waited for you to step off the curb, and I, pretending it was a high mountain, jumped off, holding tight to your hand as we crossed the street. Do you remember that? Do you remember all those lovely walks on quiet Berkeley streets with your fidgity girl who always wanted to run?

Are you thinking about death now? Did you think about death much during the past years, the past weeks with us? You must have. I wish you could wake up and talk to me. We could talk now, Mother. Now that you know death is near; I can see it in your face. Death is present and accepted and neither of us has anything to defend or attack, and we could talk now.

I could tell you things that I couldn't say otherwise. I could afford to tell you how many ways you are right, at the same time that you are wrong. I could relax and agree with you.

You are right about my marriage. Bob is ambitious and sturdy, but not intelligent. He is not honest enough to be intelligent. He has never changed, never been different from the driving, determined boy who wanted to be an advertising tycoon. Instead he became an education tycoon. Do you know, I think now that he has always been a little deaf? The ailments of our middle age are made by us in our youth. He has never really heard what I was saying. Why do you suppose he pretended to listen?

You are right about my children too. There we are alike, in our feelings about our children. Are there any parents who are not disappointed in their children? It must be in our nature to mistake biology for immortality, to look for a continuing thread between us and our children, a connection that doesn't exist.

But suppose our disappointment is no mistake. Suppose the world is really getting worse and worse, and each generation is worse than the one before? How can I think such thoughts? If I were in your place, if I knew I was dying, now, right now, would I just let go and let myself think such thoughts? But I am dying, just as you are, we are all dying. If we let ourselves remember that we are all dying we might be capable of thinking anything.

Looking at my death, I would look at the truth of my life and agree with you again. All my life is a waste of time, a waste of energy. I run around sticking my finger into holes in the dike, but all is collapsing, and the flood is coming. I look at you and think this, but when I leave here I will go on the same. Habit is strong, and I am already old, just as you are, too old to change habits. I will go on just as I have with political work and community projects, without believing in a thing I do, just as I have believed in nothing for... for so long a time that I am just not sure when I stopped believing. I confess that to you now. I have no more believed in the worth of all these things I do than you have. I go on doing them because I can't refuse the people who ask. I cannot tell them, no, and tell them why I say no. I cannot destroy their hope too. I do personal favors for people who ask. Nothing more. Nothing.

And I don't mind doing it, passing around meaningless petitions, collecting money to be misused. Only one thing really bothers me. What bothers me is being praised for doing it. How I squirm when one of my friends, my good, loyal friends, says what a wonderful woman I am to go on in the face of defeat after defeat. Then I feel dishonest. Then I feel hypocritical and dirty.

The only person who doesn't believe in my superiority, my dedication, is Gary. Oh, how he sees through me. I feel him watching me and I know what he is thinking, though he never says anything, not anymore. How you two hate each other! Your feelings toward each other must be the most real feelings, the strongest feelings, in the house. And how much you agree in your opinion of me. How is it that you two never seemed to see how much you agree?

I suppose you classified Gary among all my stupid, futile causes. But there you are wrong. Gary is real, a real person. He stands full and solid against the background made up of all my silly little activities and shows them up for what they are. It was hard, at first, for me to accept that, but I think he is helping me to see things more clearly.

Do I have to, must I really see it all so clearly?

Shall I make one last confession to you, Mother? Now that you are in that kindest, most objective state. There is a cruel, selfish, childish part of me that wishes...almost...that Gary were still in prison. I miss his letters. I miss the pure love of the words sent between us, the pure understanding of each other's suffering. I miss the certainty I felt in that one small area of understanding. I miss the longing I felt to rescue him and free him. I miss his gratitude. Most shameful of all, I miss his utter dependence on me.

You sigh.

Have you heard any of my thoughts? Are you someplace, on the edge of somewhere, where everything is clear, everything is finally understood and accepted?

The nurse brings me a chair. I will sit here with you. I will sit and watch, and hope, for a sign that there is such a clear place and that you are there and that I may be, we all may be there, sometime.

The nurse brings me coffee. She sees me as that rare, devoted daughter who will not leave her mother's bedside. No, I am not devoted, only watchful, waiting for the sign. Waiting for the sign that what I am now, how I feel, all the wasted hopes and unanswered questions, finally are all swept into some place where they come together into a knowable pattern. For, if this isn't true, then my life is scraps and bits that only drift about until the light simply goes out and they are lost and forgotten in the dark.

Which is it, Mother? Show me a sign that you are beginning to know something now, that something is knowable.

* * *

"DO YOU TREAT all women like whores, or just me?"

I turn over and look at her. Without clothes on, Barbara looks younger, a little fat, but her skin is smoother on her body than on her face. She knows it, the way she stretches out there uncovered. A woman shouldn't just lay there, so loose and bare, like...she looks at my face and pulls the sheet up to her chin.

"At first," she says, lights a cigarette, inhales and blows out the smoke, "I thought you finished fast because you hadn't been with a woman for a long time. But you still do it."

"Do what?"

"Rush. You're all through in five minutes. Before I even get started. You know..." She touches my shoulder. "...it's nice to take our time. Haven't you ever heard of..." She takes her hand away. "You don't like to be touched, do you?"

"I don't know."

"You're all taut and stiff, even right after making love."

I don't answer her.

She sighs. "And...anything I say makes you think I'm just a dirty old lady. All men are either impotent or puritans or both." She laughs. "That was a joke, a joke on me. Why can't you laugh?"

"I don't see anything funny."

She raises herself on her elbow. One breast hangs, resting on the bed. Funny how a woman's breasts change shape every time they move. I wonder what it's like to have breasts. Seems sloppy, those bags hanging in front of your chest.

"I bet..." She inhales, then blows the smoke in my face. "...oh, sorry. I bet you've never had an orgasm in your life. I mean, you ejaculate, but I bet you never had a real orgasm."

If she says much more, I'm going to hit her.

"Gary, look, don't be angry. I'm not trying to embarrass you, I'm just trying to...reach you." She falls on her back again and just lays there. Christ, now she's crying. No noise, just those streams going from the corner of her eyes back to her ears.

"What in hell are you crying about now?"

"Just...my life. The conditions of my life. The trap."

"You don't know what a trap is."

"Oh, yes, I forgot." She sighs. "You have a monopoly on suffering."

"Lady, I know what real traps are. I know what it means to be born into a trap, and to beat your head against the walls without even knowing that's what you're doing."

I stop, and she sighs, then nods. "Go on. Get it off your chest."

"Get what off?"

"That's your real orgasm. You need to go on talking about it. That's the way we always end up. That's all right. I don't mind listening, if you need it."

"I don't need anything. Christ, you're worse than Sally. She tells me, forget it all, start new, and you tell me to get it off my chest. It's all the same thing, isn't it?"

142

Silence again for a while.

"Tell me why you disapprove of me," she says. "Is it sex? Is it because I'm 'an easy lay'? Is that it?"

"You want me to say yes so you can call me a puritan again."

"And you want an excuse to be angry at me instead of feeling guilty for taking advantage of me."

"You're crazy."

"It happens all the time. Men shove me into bed, then feel guilty, so they start some kind of argument with me, then they can walk away with me screaming at them, and they feel better."

"Taking advantage, shit! I'm the paid help, services on demand, having trouble satisfying the Lady of the House. But at these prices..."

"Gary!"

"Shit! Who's treated like a whore? You think you can..."

"Gary, I never thought of you as..."

"What do you mean, you never thought of me as anything else!" She's just shaking her head, shaking and shaking it and biting her lip. "So I'm getting a lousy three bucks an hour to..."

"To work in the garden! And you haven't done much of that!"

"My other duties keep me from it. And I don't think three bucks an hour is enough for..."

"I don't know why you're doing this." She keeps biting her lip. "You're pushing, pushing, trying to start some awful fight. God, maybe it is my fault. I ought to be stronger. I ought to be like Sally...get myself together and put my energy into something worthwhile, if only I could...you're trying to make me hate you, make me throw you out."

"Go ahead. My life doesn't depend on your lousy three bucks an hour."

"I never said it did. And I never said that sex was part of...good God, you must know that a shortage of sex isn't one of my problems. A shortage of everything else, tenderness, kindness, meaning...I thought we would be kind to each other...I thought..."

"You never thought in your life, or you wouldn't be here..."

"...with you. Is that why you hate me? Do you hate yourself so much that you hate anyone who would touch you?"

She's asking for it. She looks at my fist, then at my face. She waits. I get up and start to put my clothes on.

"I'm not throwing you out, Gary. I'm not going to do whatever it is you want. You can go work in the garden, there's still an hour or two of daylight left."

"Fuck your garden."

"And me."

"No more."

"Small loss."

"You people think you can buy anything, you don't buy my balls for three bucks an hour."

"You people...what people? I never tried to do anything but help you."

"Save it. Help yourself. You're the one who needs it."

"You're right. But sometimes we can't do it all for ourselves. We need other people. Even you, Gary."

"I don't need you." I've got my clothes on now, and she's standing in front of me with nothing on. She acts like she doesn't know she's naked.

"You can't go on hating anyone who tries to help you."

"I don't."

"You do. You even hate Sally. You hate her most of all."

"Shut up!"

"You hate Sally. You hate the best people you know. You hate them the most. You hate Sally more than you hate me!"

Then I hit her. Harder than I meant to. She falls back, but the bed is there. She falls on the bed. Then she sits up with her hand over her eye. She nods. Slowly. "All right," she says. "You win." She keeps nodding. "Get out."

* * *

WE SIT in front of the fire, Sam and Bob and I. John lies on the floor in the corner playing with one of the cats. He looks as languid as the cat, with none of the cat's potential to spring. And I, still in my robe, at noon on a Sunday, like an invalid. Bob faces me, on the edge of his chair.

"It was a nice service. People there we haven't seen for years. Haven't seen Cyd since the Henry Wallace days."

I blow on my coffee. "Nothing to bring them all together again, except for death. Some of those people have been holding a wake for years."

Bob bites his lips uneasily as he watches me. "A great many people love you, Sally. All the people who came to the service. That was a tribute to you. All your friends."

"Seeing all of them appear...like old ghosts...that was what depressed me. I wasn't sad about Mother. She was old and she died. That's all."

"You're not yourself."

How he fidgets. "Put it down to menopause. Middle-age crisis. Everyone goes through it, they say. Even men. Though it manifests itself differently with them. Like maybe chasing younger women, having an affair. That way isn't so often open to aging women. Too bad. It sounds like fun." Sam and John are still as statues. Everyone knew, Bob, didn't you know that?

He puts his hand on mine. His hand trembles. "Huh?" Suddenly he's deaf. Come on, Bob. Blurt it out. Say, yes, I've been sleeping with Millie, and it does help, can you stand it a bit longer, Sally? God, I could respect you if you could say that, if you could come straight out with it.

"I guess you won't feel in the mood to do much about Christmas."

"Why shouldn't I? I love Christmas. I'm going to have it no matter what happens. I had Christmas through years of war. People die all the time all over the world, and we still have Christmas. I'll get the tree today."

"All right. What about Christmas dinner? Who should we invite?"

"The usual bunch, I guess. And Millie, of course."

I expect his hand to shake again, but he's calm, as if he's glad I mentioned her. "She won't be here. She's got a job in San Diego. Leaving at the end of this week." He raises his eyes and looks into mine. Level. Straight. Not bad. Not good enough. She ended it, not you. He gets up. "By the way, I'm afraid I had a run-in with Gary. Not very serious. Just that when he refused to come to the services, I..."

"Why should he have come? My mother was nothing to him. You're not asking me to get rid of him?" An exchange? If Millie goes, Gary goes? "I couldn't do that, you know. It's a condition of his parole."

Bob is shaking his head. "No, he can stay here as long as you want him. Just don't let him...well, I don't think he's good for you."

"In what way?"

"His hostility, his bitterness."

Oh, no you don't, you can't blame it on Gary. "I think he's much better since Thanksgiving. Besides, he's hardly here anymore now that he has settled down to writing. When he's not in his room, he's working for Barbara or Sam, and practically every night he goes to see Dennis. I see no reason why he shouldn't go on this way indefinitely. Do you, Sam?"

I've looked in the wrong direction for support. Sam looks uncomfortable. He hesitates, then says quietly, "I'm afraid I wouldn't know. I've seen very little of him."

"You mean he hasn't been working for you?"

"Just one day last month," says Sam, "and half a day about two weeks ago. He agreed to come early the next morning for a concrete pour. He never showed up. Left me in a bind."

"That's two down, counting the Meyers." John is lying on his back, holding the cat straight up in his two hands. Poor Molly hangs patient and limp, her head twisting around to look for escape.

"He wasn't a bad worker," says Sam, "but he didn't like it. Some people can't say no. They make others say it for them. Not being able to count on him, I couldn't hire him again."

"Oh, Sam, I'm sorry."

Sam smiles at me. "Sometimes I wonder how the old Quakers felt about the escaped slaves they helped along the Underground Railway. Did they find some of them selfish, dirty, violent, immoral? You know, sometimes when I'm counseling, I suddenly realize I really don't like some of the young men I'm trying to help. The older I get, the more I feel we should just assume everyone we meet is a little crazy, until proven otherwise." No one answers. Sam is in one of his rare, talkative moods, and we don't want to interrupt. "Gary reminds me of my first wife," he says with a thoughtful smile. "She used to do things like that. I was very patient because I thought she couldn't help it. I don't know how long it took me to realize that she was trying to infuriate me. By the time I understood that, she was...so enraged by my lack of response, that there was nothing left but her hatred of me. When she threw me out, she said I'd driven her to it, and she didn't know how she'd stood me so long."

"Well, now the only person who hasn't complained about him is Barbara," says Bob.

"And Dennis," I say quickly. "He goes to see Dennis every night, almost, for help with his writing.''

"Or that's where he says he goes,'' says John.

"Where he goes is none of your business!'' Of course, everyone knows I'm not defending Gary but attacking John because he has already dropped out of college. With a fine list of reasons. We seem to have given our children only one thing, a supply of rationalizations for their refusal to try, just to try.

Sam looks at his watch. "I have a favor to ask. I wouldn't bring it up at a time like this, but. . .''

"It is a pretty bad time,'' Bob says. "Not only the loss of Sally's mother, but. . .well, with all the Gary complications. . .and. . .Sally's been pushing herself too hard for a long time, and I think she might just need to. . .''

"Never mind!'' The kind of support I needed from you, My Dear, is not this late pat on the head, not this old, uneasy man left over after his last fling. "What is it, Sam?''

"Most of the men I'm counseling are deserters. It's very tricky. They're usually in a desperate state. First thing to do is to calm them down. Then they can listen, think about their alternatives. Make a decision. That's where you come in. If they decide to turn themselves in, we sometimes need a place for them to stay overnight, one night, at the most two, waiting to be picked up. Preferably a quiet, natural, reassuring place, a real home. . .like yours.''

"But aren't they fugitives? Wouldn't that be. . .''

I wave my hand to hush Bob, and Sam shakes his head.

"I keep the ones who have decided to go underground or leave the country. I'm only asking you to keep the ones who have already called the FBI and reported themselves. Just a place to sleep. Sometimes they need an older woman around.''

"And they'd be picked up here?''

"No, no. I take them to the Quaker Meeting House for that.''

Another finger in the dike, a stayover place for a man on his way to prison. Is that all I can offer? A place to wait. "Of course, Mother's room is empty. Bring anyone you like.''

Sam stands up. "Thank you. I may not have to bother you at all. Or three months from now I may need a place on five minutes notice. It'll be nice to know I can count on you. As usual.'' Sam shakes my hand and leaves without another word. He seems to walk so softly, as if hardly letting his weight down upon the earth. I look into the fire again.

"Yeah," says John, "you better stick to political cons; they're a better class of people."

"Better than who?" I feel my hand twitching. If my precious son were closer, I could slap his pompous face. "There is no reason why Gary should work at something he doesn't want to do."

"Except to support himself."

"I know other young men who feel no compunction at all about not supporting themselves!" Silence. Bob is watching me closely, as if to confirm that I have really lost patience with John. John puts the cat down and leaves the room.

"And Gary does work! He works at writing. Why shouldn't he take the opportunity to do the work he wants to do? It doesn't hurt us. He doesn't eat much. We hardly see him. I admire him. I admire Gary for knowing what he wants to do and doing it, for not acquiescing meekly to every meaningless demand or expectation and frittering away his life in pointless trivialities!" I'm suddenly blinking back tears.

Bob keeps squinting at me and leaning forward. Looking tired. Looking old. "I've been thinking about what you said."

"What?"

"About the teaching machines. I think you're right. It's all a gimmick. If I get a sabbatical, I should work on something else. Something real. Maybe we can talk about it later. Maybe you'll have some ideas."

I shake my head. No ideas.

"But you'll think of something," Bob says. "You always do. Anything good, any good ideas in my life, always have come from you."

I can't seem to do anything but shake my head. What do I want, blood? The man is trying to make it up. Can't I give a little?

He smiles desperately. "Hey, how about that tree? Aren't we going out to get that Christmas tree?"

I nod. I try to smile back at him. "In a little while. I'll get up and dressed. Not just yet. Later."

* * *

MUST BE pretty late. It's light outside. I was going to get up at seven. Did that alarm clock go off? I guess it did. I remember. I heard the alarm. I dreamed I got up, sat down to the typewriter and wrote a long poem. It went on and on, pages and pages. It contained everything, told everything. It flowed out. God, it was beautiful. What was it about? How did it start? If I could just remember the first line. I have to keep pencil and paper in bed with me, the way I used to in my bunk. So when I woke up in the middle of the night with an idea, I could get it down before I forgot. Trouble is, none of those ideas was worth a damn. I never could use one of them. But, at least, when I woke up hearing all those bastards coughing or yelling or the guards making as much light and noise as they could, I'd grab my paper and pencil and tell myself, Goddammit, you woke up because you're inspired. It didn't matter what I wrote down, just so I wrote something, did something.

Nine-thirty. I better take a piss and get some coffee. Don't want to take time to eat. Or talk. Hope they don't . . . sounds quiet up there.

Everybody gone? Cats, sitting in the sun, dozing. Sally's note on the table. She writes a book before she takes off every day. Where is she today? In court. Those black dudes in Richmond. "Someone turn the oven on at four." Two phone messages for Bob and . . . here, there's the coffee for me on the stove. Okay.

Might as well take the whole pot down with me. Cup. Sugar. Got everything? Okay. Down, down. Careful, don't drop the pot.

Coffee beside the typewriter. Paper rolled in. Okay. For the next two hours, nothing can interrupt me. Can't even hear the phone down here.

How white the paper is. Gets whiter every day. Finish one cup of coffee before I start. Need hot, hot coffee to warm that cold spot at the pit of my stomach. I look at that white paper and the cold spot in my stomach gets colder, like that white paper is cold snow, coming in through my eyes and sinking down into me. What did Dennis say about that writer who killed himself because he couldn't face that piece of blank, white paper in the typewriter every morning?

Well, I can't just sit here and look at the damned paper. Come on, do something.

What was I going to write? Elegy for Sylvester. Right. How do I start?

       Slam your soul against the bars

That's good, that's good. His son, the little baby, was his soul. All men put their soul in their kid. I guess. Except he wasn't sure this kid was his. Well, put that in too, that was part of what was driving him crazy. No, for the poem it's better if the kid is his, his soul battered to death on prison bars. You can't say everything in a poem. But that guy was crazy before he ever came in, anyone could see that. Can I put that in somewhere? He was crazy and they put him in so they could push him over, all the way over the edge. They. Who? Everybody, all crazy, crazier than Sylvester. Deep, the insanity, so deep...

Where was I? How did everything I wanted to say get so complicated? Just that one incident, that's all, just to show that clear...and it got so complicated. One lousy line. And it's...ten-thirty already. Christ, it's all there, all inside, and all I squeeze out is one line. I'm out, I'm free, and I can write what I want, when I want, and it's like I'm closed up tighter than I was, bottled up, nothing coming out. Maybe I'm just kidding myself. Maybe there's nothing inside.

Not true, not true. It came pouring out of me the past year. What stopped it? What's wrong? Why should it be harder to write here? What's different?

Well, Christ, I was half out of my mind there. And what else was there to do, just to drown out the sound and stink of everybody else going out of their heads too.

Maybe I should try the tape recorder again. I can talk into it, try lines, just say things that come into my head. Talking's easier than writing. Writing feels permanent, like you put it down and see how stupid it is right here, staring at you.

Oh, there's still some of my old poems on the tape. I can listen a while, get a feel for it. Yeah. Right. That was a good one. My voice sure sounds funny. Oh. I don't like that one anymore.

Okay. Now

"Slam your soul against the bars."

What next? Watching that spool spin away the tape makes me just as nervous as looking at the damned paper in the typewriter.

"Oh, shit."

Wait. I know. I never worked at the typewriter or tape recorder. I sat on my bunk with paper and a pencil. That's it, I didn't punch the words, I drew them with my hand, sitting up? no, laying down, knees up, paper on my knees, on a book. Where's that fucking pencil? Where's that book I had? Not stiff enough.

Up the stairs. Must be pencils on the dining room table with all the other junk.

Here's a good soft one, take two just in case. A book? Good stiff one, here. Got everything?

A little wine might help. Just a little. It's mine anyway. I bought it to replace the stuff I drank. They haven't touched it. Probably don't like this brand. Used to seeing the old lady up here, stiff and staring at me when I came up for coffee or wine. I almost miss her. Now it's only me and the cats.

Down again. Careful. Trip and you lose a whole bottle of wine. Down. No wonder they call my room The Dungeon.

Now. Pillow under my head. Knees up, book, paper, pencil. One swallow of wine. Well, two swallows. Cork it, roll it under the bed. That's it. That's better.

Maybe I should write about the old lady. Or Barbara. Keep thinking about some of the things that stupid broad said to me. Grist for the mill. Like Dennis says, she's just something to put in a poem. No. She's not important. I can only write about suffering people. What does she know about suffering, what do any of them know? I'll make them know, I'll push it in their faces and rub it in. And some day Sally'll be talking to people and she'll say that with all the running around do-gooding she did there was only one thing she did ever amounted to anything, and that was getting Gary Wilson out of prison and letting him live in her house till his first book of poems was published and became the first poetry best seller.

All I have to do is write one poem a day. Just one. That's 365 in one year. That's more than a life's work for most poets. Okay, some might not be so good, throw out a hundred and there's still 265. At the end of a year, I can leave here, live on royalties, then ease up, write maybe 100 poems a year from then on. Do I want to go on those TV talk shows? I think I'll just refuse. No. Fuck them. On the other hand, I could do a lot of good, tell about prison.

But if Dennis is right, there's no money in poetry, no talk shows, no nothing.

Where the hell is that bottle? Here. No, that's an empty. Here. Just a sip. Might as well leave it here. No sense crawling around under the bed for it.

The real money is in non-fiction, prison expose. But that territory's gone over. After Malcolm X and Eldridge Cleaver, the vultures moved in on that, the professionals, like that friend of Sally's who wrote that book on prisons. "Do you want to meet her?" Shit.

What's wrong, don't I think it's a good book? Maybe I can tell her where she went wrong? Shit. There's nothing wrong, she got all her facts and told it. But what right does she have? She took it away from me. What right does some English bitch in Oakland have to make money out of. . .

Envy. Okay, so it's envy. I want to write the books, and make the money, and be interviewed and get famous. I want to write them all.

The fiction angle has possibilities. Even Dennis said I should get back to the novel I started. The time could be just right for it. It all depends on whether the movies pick it up. You have to write it so it can be transferred to the screen with no trouble. (Dennis looked like he had heartburn when I said that.) If the movies pick it up I'm set for life and I can write whatever I want for the rest of my life, or write nothing, or. . .where did I put it? Christ, it must be at the bottom of this box. I have to get this stuff sorted out. Go through it all, send out what looks publishable, and then get going on that novel again.

Why did I stop? I was about halfway through. Sally thought it was good. She's not the best judge. She thinks it's just great anybody manages to write a book, it's all just great to her.

Why did I stop halfway? Well, I got out. No, it was before I got out. I stopped. Something went wrong, like I ran out of steam, it was all there, but nowhere to go. What did Dennis say? A novel is different from a poem. Brilliant, so what else is new? He went on a long time about that, something about the energy sources to keep you going all the way through a novel. I don't remember anything he said though. I was half asleep in front of the fire, dozing with that good brandy. He's all right, for a fag. But he made writing a novel sound like building a skyscraper without a blueprint. What does he know about it? He quit writing because he's no good. He said so himself.

How do I know he's no good? He never showed me anything he ever wrote. Maybe he's no good, but he could be ten times better than me and still not be good enough. Maybe I'm no good either.

And that's why it's almost three o'clock and I've written one lousy, fucking line. And I've got to get out of here before Sally gets home and I have to explain to her that, no, I don't want to eat dinner with her and Bob and John, and then have to watch her smile and say, ''How's the writing?''

But at least now I know what I have to do. Get that novel out and finish it. And a poem a day. Short one. Why not? A novel and 365 poems by the end of the year. Sooner on the novel, it's already half done.

I'll start tomorrow morning.

Seven, no six o'clock. I'll set the alarm and this time I'll get right up.

Tomorrow.

* * *

POOR BARBARA. I always seem to be saying poor Barbara. I hang up. Then I look at the phone as if it will ring again and she will tell me about another new disaster. No, that was today's disaster. Enough. I will go back to the living room and get on with the tree.

Just like Bob to bring home this huge thing and then leave me to decorate it. My God, I'm sounding like Mother again. Stop it. Stop. I must stop punishing him. I don't mean to. Then forget it. It's all over. I'm trying. Then try harder. A minor infidelity won't wreck a marriage, but holding a grudge will. Try. I'm tired. That's all it is. Keep hanging things on the tree. Yes. In a few minutes Bob will be back with the extra lights, and...there he is now. Smile.

"Oh, Gary, it's you. How do you like the tree?" I shouldn't have asked. I can tell by the way he looks at it, and then looks at me, he disapproves of all this Christmas fuss. "I know you think I shouldn't when the world is so..." He shrugs. "Oh, you're like John, you'll both sneer at it, but you'll enjoy it when it's all lit up."

"I bet you sent out Christmas cards too."

"Yes."

"To prisoners too?"

I nod. At least that should please him

"Getting a Christmas card in prison is really getting a knife twisted in your gut."

I look at him. "But that's not how you felt when..." He's not looking at me. Maybe it was the way he felt. Maybe he felt both things at once, the knife in his gut and the hand reaching out to help him.

If we were still writing to each other, I'd write and tell Gary about the tree and he'd read my letter over and over again, imagining it, enjoying it. But now that he is actually here, in front of an actual tree, he can't enjoy it, and if he keeps acting this way, neither will I.

"Gary, why do you suppose..." No, I won't say anything about it. I can tell he doesn't like to be reminded of our letters. I've become very nostalgic about them. I miss writing them, stealing those few minutes alone whenever I could, writing down my feelings and knowing that he was waiting to read about them, about anything I had to say.

"What?" His voice is so harsh.

"Never mind. How's..." No, don't ask about his writing. Obviously it's very hard, going very badly, creative people have such an awful time. He hates being asked about it. Don't look at him, just keep hanging ornaments and making small talk. Sometimes when I do that he forgets to be stiff and serious. "Barbara called and told me what happened." What a strange look on his face. "Didn't you know? Oh, I thought this was your day to work there." No answer. Stiff. Oh, God, he's probably had a fight with her too. Well, I knew it would happen. He just doesn't want to do that kind of work. His face is absolutely weird, unreadable. What on earth is he thinking? "Her house was burglarized. Her stereo, television, a pearl ring that belonged to her mother, a piece of African sculpture. In fact, each little thing that was of the slightest value. They knew just what to take. Worst of all, there was no sign of a search, nothing messed up. They knew what she had and where everything was. It was someone she knew, I'm sure. Someone who'd been in the house. She had an identifying number stenciled on everything just in case the police recover anything, but..."

"Bitch! Lousy bitch!"

"What...what is it?" He looks absolutely mad. "Gary, what..."

"I knew she'd figure out a way to get back at me. I suppose the police are on their way here!"

"No, why should they be on their way..."

He looks at me as if my stupidity is more than he can bear. "They asked her who's been in the house, and she..."

"Oh, Gary, for heaven's sake, no one is accusing you!" I sit back on my heels. I feel as if he hit me.

He laughs. His mouth looks so ugly. "Oh, no, no one has to accuse me, just mention my name, that's enough to..."

"No one mentioned your name. I'm sure...do you want me to call her back and ask? Barbara is smarter than I about things like that. She'd make a point of not mentioning you, I'm sure. I'll call her. What do you mean, she'd figure a way to get back at you? What did you..."

He walks behind me, toward the fireplace, kicking a box of ornaments as he moves.

"Did you have an argument with her?" I sigh because I know the answer already. "Maybe your work wasn't satisfactory."

"That's right." I've never seen such a nasty smile. "That's right, my...work wasn't satisfactory."

Oh, God. And I thought, because she wasn't talking about anyone, that she was...making do alone for a while. How stupid of me. Of course, Gary is just the type: young, lost, angry. She attracts them like sugar, left out unwatched, uncovered, overrun by ants. Can't blame the ants. Or the sugar. I sigh. "You needn't worry, Barbara isn't vindictive. But I understand how you would fear the police..."

"No, you don't. You never could in a million years. You don't know anything about it."

"All right." If I don't cut him off now I'll get another lecture. "I probably don't understand as I would if I had experienced it, but..."

"You think you do. That's the trouble with you people, you think you know everything. But you don't. Six months in my shoes and you'd learn something about..."

"All right, Gary, I don't want another sermon."

"Sermon."

"Yes, really, I'm too tired to listen to more tirades on how little I know or understand or appreciate. I sympathize with you, but..."

"No one wants your sympathy."

Oh, my head hurts. Suddenly, like a great rock, a headache has fallen on me. "Gary, I don't want to fight with you." He just glares at me. "But you seem determined to. You hang over us, glowering, waiting for the storm to break. Don't you see what you're doing? First the Meyers, then Sam, then Barbara. Shutting the door on people who try to help..."

"Their kind of help is..."

"And now me. Now that you've settled in, you have a place to write, food, time...what else do you want?"

"I want to feel like a human being."

"What have we said or done that makes you feel less?"

"It's not what you say or do, it's what you are!"

My neck is hurting from bending back and looking up at him as he stands there, the fire glowing behind him, tall and dark like a shadow in front of the fire. It's dark outside now, only the few lights on the tree glow. They seem pitiful, small and tired, like me, not really up to the job.

"What are we, Gary? What are we that you hate so much? Don't say it, I know, middle-class, right? But that's just a word. That doesn't mean anything. We don't have much money, if that's what it means. And this wreck of a house is as bad structurally as any slum. And why do you despise my friends? The Meyers, yes, they have money. But they're sort of outcasts, aren't they, with so much they've never been allowed to give. And Sam...Sam works with his hands, doesn't he? And Barbara...you know, Barbara is less secure than you, and makes less money than you...than you could if you wanted to. And Dennis knows plenty about oppression and prejudice and..."

"You really believe that shit!" he yells. I go on shaking my head as he shouts at me. "You really do. You all think you're out of The System because you sign a few petitions and give away some money and because somebody called you a name once or twice. But you're in it. You're safe. You need it. If that system you're always saying you're against should change, you'd be screwed, you'd really be in trouble. You wouldn't know what to do. Then you'd learn, you'd understand what I'm trying to say!"

I just keep shaking my head.

"Look. Let's put Barbara against...my mother. If my mother loses her job, it's all over. She goes from a mansion in Pacific Heights back to the housing project. Lines up for Welfare, if she can get it. Humiliation and filth. But Barbara, look at Barbara. She hasn't even got a steady job. But she's still in that house on the hill. It's hers. Okay, she hasn't anything else. But she goes to dinner at the Meyers' house, and they lend her their Claremont Card so she can swim at their club, and her other friends have a place at Squaw Valley where she can go and ski, and she can trade houses with that teacher she knows in France, and spend the summer there, and...let's say she even lost that house. Where would she go? She could stay here for a while, or with other friends...while Jake is using his contacts to get her another job and Judy finds her a bargain house, or a mansion she can babysit for a year while the owner goes to Europe...Christ, you people are so far in it you can't see it, how the whole thing is set up to take care of you and to let other people drop to the bottom."

"Like you."

"Like me."

"But you didn't drop to the bottom, because I *did* know you could, and I wanted to catch you and not let you..."

"You want me to bow, you want gratitude? How do you want it, on my knees?"

"The question is, what do *you* want? You hate all of us because we're middle-class. Because of our status. Well, young man, without that status of mine you hate, you'd still be in prison. Make up your mind. You can't have it both ways! And I'm damned if I'm going to apologize to you for what I am!" My throat has suddenly caught and closed. I'm hoarse. How did this happen? It's what he wants. He wants me screaming at him. He wants me to throw him out. Then who'll be left? Dennis? How will he make poor, sweet Dennis angry?

"Go on. Might as well say it all." He smiles hatefully.

"I don't know what's wrong with you. You called it pride. I call it mean and stupid. You're full of hate. You feed on hate. The only time you look alive is when you're angry, raging. Sometimes I think you'd rather be back in prison than here, just so you'd have every excuse to hate!" And I'm crying. My voice is a whisper, and I'm croaking and crying like an old woman. "I knew most of what I did was ineffective. I never pretended I was changing the world. I told you that. In our letters. That's why I wanted to help you, singly, individually, to do something meaningful. And you hate me because I helped you!"

"Christ, people like you have a nerve. Christ! You got me paroled to you so that you could feel you were effective. So you could feel your life was meaningful. Christ, didn't I have enough trouble without having to supply a fucking meaning to your fucking life!"

* * *

"OH, YOU'RE EARLY. I was just about to fix myself some dinner. Want some?"

I shake my head, and Dennis pulls the door open wide to let me in. He's wearing a white turtle neck sweater over worn tan cords. Face looks darker, rich color, above the white. He shuts the front door and follows me into the front room. I face one of the big book cases, not seeing it, too close to read titles, not wanting to see them, not see anything.

"Maybe you'd prefer a drink."

I turn and nod. He's smiling gently. Kind of sad. Not a bad smile.

"Okay, you know where it is. But I won't join you tonight. I have to lay off. We sit here talking and I don't notice how much I'm drinking, but the next morning. . . what's wrong?''

I don't answer him. I go to the kitchen and get a bottle of wine and a glass. When I come back into the front room, he's lighting the stuff in the fireplace. Then he steps back and sits down in his leather chair. He motions to the other chair, but I can't sit down. I pour a glass of wine and drink it down, then another, then put the bottle and glass down on a little table. I keep walking back and forth. I can't stop. He doesn't say anything. He just waits.

"Well, I'm all through at Sally's."

"I don't understand. Did she ask you to leave?''

I shake my head. "Not exactly.''

"But you had an argument.''

"Yes.''

"About your drinking?''

I shake my head again. Then, "Well, I guess that's part of it.''

"What else was the argument about?''

"Everything. Nothing. I don't know. It was just. . .'' I'm stopped for a minute trying to remember what the argument really was about, how it got started. "It's crazy but I can't remember what set it off.''

"Well," he's saying, "I'm sure you'll patch it up. It's not easy for people to live together, but Sally thinks the world of you and she's such a great person I can't imagine her holding it against you that. . .''

"I can't go back there! You don't understand anything about it.''

"Tell me, and I'll try.''

"I've screwed up with all of them. Not only Sally.''

"Bob?''

"Oh, he always hated me. No, I mean the Meyers, Barbara, Sam. You're the only person left that I can talk to.'' He doesn't say anything, but he looks a little more worried, like he can finally see it's serious. "You knew about what happened with the Meyers.''

He nods.

"You all talked about it.''

"At Thanksgiving. I hadn't really talked to you yet, and that was the first I knew things weren't going well. But I just assumed, everyone assumed, you were having trouble adjusting to being free.''

Free. I feel like hitting him for using that word. "Then I messed things up with the others.'' I tell him about Sam, then about Barbara. Talking about Barbara makes me mad. "That dumb broad.''

158

He's looking into the fire, as if he doesn't want to look at my face. "Why did you do it?"

"Screw her?"

"Quarrel with her...she's a pretty weak opponent to take on."

"I don't know." He doesn't seem to understand why I'm so mad at her. Maybe because he's queer.

"Why'd you let Sam down? That was a pretty good job."

"I don't know."

So he just sits looking at the fire and I keep walking up and down, and neither of us says anything for a long time. "Christ, I just hate these middle-class liberals doing me favors."

"I'm a middle-class liberal."

"No, you can't be, you're..." He's out in two ways, but I guess I'd better only mention one. "...black."

"Sam's not middle-class. He's escaped all categories. He's..."

"Yeah, I know, a god-damned saint. Well, I'm not. Look at him, sweating his life away to pay alimony. So he had one big moment in his life thirty years ago, and what did it all add up to? He's a slave."

"I don't think he sees it that way."

"The guy's crazy."

"You sound angry at him too."

"That's what Sally says. She says I hate anyone who tries to help me. Maybe she's right. Not at first, but gradually, after a while, something builds up in me. I can't stand them. I feel like I have to get away from them, like I can't breathe."

"Why?"

"Christ, I don't know."

More silence. I take another glass of wine.

"Why *do* you drink so much?"

I turn around, ready for the fight. But there's nothing in his face but curiosity.

"I don't know."

"Have you been drinking a long time?"

"Ever since I knew what it was and could get hold of it."

He nods. "You drink like an Indian. I used to teach in an Indian school. The boys poured huge, murderous quantities of the stuff down them. I realized liquor meant something very different to them than it did to other people. I've thought a lot about it. People who practice ecstatic religions, you know, usually take to alcohol that way. Know what I mean?"

159

I don't know what he's talking about. "For me it just eases. . ."

"Pain?"

"No. No, it's not pain. What I feel is. . .like a motor racing inside me, a big, roaring airplane motor, grinding away in me, spinning and grinding, while I'm trying to stand still and think. Drinking slows it down so I. . .oh, shit, why talk about it." I pour another glass of wine and drink it, just to show him he didn't make me self-conscious about it.

"What happened between you and Sally?"

I shrug. "Just a stupid misunderstanding. But then it got bigger, and I said a lot of things. The funny thing is I kept thinking, while I was yelling at her, that this would screw me up for good, that if I said these things, I'd have to go. But I went ahead and said them anyway."

"Without believing what you were saying?"

"Some of it I believed. Some of it I didn't." If he asks me which was which, I won't be able to say.

"And she threw you out?"

I shake my head. "I walked out before she could say it. But don't tell me I can go back. I can't."

"What are you going to do?"

"Christ, I don't know." Now I finally sit down in the leather chair. I'm tired and a little dizzy from the wine. I forgot to eat today. "What do you think?"

"What do I think you should do?"

"No, no. What do you think about. . .what I've already done, about. . .all this mess."

He reaches for a pipe. I knew he'd have to do that. He picks out a pipe, fills and tamps, fills and tamps, finally lights it, puffs, takes it out, puffs, then leans back. It takes him about five minutes, and I guess it's how he thinks, giving himself time to put all his thoughts together before he says something he really means. Or maybe it's just a pose to make me think he's got something really important to say.

"I think. . .I think no one can assess the mental and moral, even physical exhaustion brought on by your writing. Not even you. That's the objection, by the way, I'd have to your drinking, the drain on your strength, though the way you describe it, maybe you can't slow down enough to write unless you do drink. If that's the case you'll have to strike some kind of balance. . ." Another two puffs. "But, just think about what this novel is taking out of you. Five, six hours a day for about a month now. God, man, nothing, not even anything that happened to you in prison, could place the strain on you that this kind of work does. There's not a lot of anything left in you, emotionally, physically. You probably. . .''

"Oh, shit!" I get up and I'm pacing back and forth again. I was afraid he'd say something like that. Okay. So he's the last one left who still gives a damn about me. Shall I keep kidding him along, or shall I let him have it. "Shit, I haven't written one damned page. Not one fucking page! Do you understand that? I come here every night talking about plot, character, tension, development, all that shit, and I haven't written two sentences.''

He doesn't say anything.

"So, you see, I let you down just like the others.''

He shrugs. "Let me down? How could you let me down?''

"Well, I'm a fake, aren't I? Writing. I haven't written a god-damned thing since I left The Farm. And I only wrote there when I couldn't think of anything else that would stop me from killing somebody. I thought I'd write when I got out. I can't.''

"Why not?''

"I just can't. I sit down in the morning. Every morning. Like I told you. That much I told you was true. But that's the only thing that was true. Didn't you wonder why I never brought anything for you to read?''

"I thought you wanted to finish the whole thing first. Some writers are like that, can't take reactions until the book is done.''

"Not me. I just never got started. I'd just sit looking at that sheet of paper. Then I'd make an outline, or add to all the outlines I already had. You should see my outlines, they'd make a thousand books, the story of the world. My plans got bigger and bigger, but I couldn't put a word to the page. I thought drinking would help, just a little, just enough to make me stop shaking every time I looked at that white paper. I'd buy a bottle when I went out, so Sally wouldn't notice. Christ, when she cleans out that room, she'll find a lot of dead soldiers under that bed.''

"Drinking didn't help, of course.''

I shook my head. "It just made me feel like I didn't care as much if I couldn't write. It made me make more plans, bigger plans, for tomorrow.''

"Why didn't you tell me?''

161

"I don't know . . . I was ashamed, I guess."

"It's nothing to be ashamed of. The greatest writers have had blocks that have lasted months, even years. There's only one thing that's harder than writing and that's not being able to write. For a writer, that is."

"And I'm a writer."

He doesn't react to that.

"You still believe in me, as a writer."

He still doesn't say anything.

"You know what I want from you?"

He nods. "You want me to tell you you have talent. I already said that."

"But then you said everyone has talent."

"You want me to tell you you're a writer. I think you are." But he frowns as if he doesn't believe what he is saying, or doesn't think I ought to believe him. "But what I think doesn't really count. The drive, the decision, has to come from inside you. I'm sorry, I'd like to say something more . . ."

"It's just that I have to believe . . . if I can't believe that all this . . . this mess . . . is because of something that has to come out of me, my . . . talent, my . . . well, if it's not that, then they're right, I'm just no good."

"I don't think it has to be one thing or the other."

"I don't want anything in between." I stand up again. "No. Nothing in between." I turn to look at him and I see a strange expression on his face, like he's studying me. "I guess I better go."

"Where will you go?"

"I don't know."

"Got any money?"

"A little."

"Here." He reaches for his wallet and pulls out a twenty. "You can pay me back sometime."

I take the bill without saying anything.

"You can rent a room somewhere for the night, then think about it, and tomorrow . . ." We walk toward the door. "You're sure you don't want something to eat?"

I shake my head, but I'm dragging my feet. It's cold out there and the wine tastes sour in my throat. I feel rotten. Because I made the big confession, told him what a mess I've made. Because I told him I'm

162

not writing. Because he's being so god-damned understanding about everything I've said. Because...

"Look, I guess..." I must look bad. He's watching me with such a worried look I can hardly stand it. "...you might as well spend the night here if you want to. Figure out your next move in the morning. There's a spare bedroom."

I don't say no. He turns and I follow him through the living room and down the short hall. On one side of the hall is his bedroom and on the other side is another one, with a big double bed. It's a bigger room than his, with a thick rug and shiny drapes. It doesn't look like the rest of the house. I bet this was the room he and his roommate slept in when he had a roommate. Now he sleeps on a narrow bed in that small, bare room. Does he keep this one ready, just in case?

"It's a king-size, long enough even for you." He laughs and pats me on the shoulder.

"Take your fucking hand off me!"

It was a reflex. It was out before I knew it. Just a made-up phrase, always ready whenever one of the queers at The Farm came at me, always with the look like I'd kill them if they messed with me. Just a reflex.

The funny thing is the way the words go through me like a shot of something, bringing me alive and sharp. And now there aren't any other words to say. Those say everything. No other words can unsay them. They were a lot more than what was needed, so they say a lot more. All I'd need to say to a pass from Dennis is, no, quiet and polite, just like him. If he made a pass. Did he? Sure he did. I believe he did. Sure, I believe it. What do his eyes say? Nothing. They're wide and blank, like somebody hit him and he's seeing stars or seeing nothing.

And now, now that we've stood here for four or five seconds, it's too late to say anything, to pretend I didn't mean it, to apologize, to explain.

So I turn and go. I stalk through the front room like he insulted me. I slam the door on my way out.

That's the last of them.

I'm free.

* * *

"NOW PRECISELY what is it this new organization does?" Jake holds the pen poised over his checkbook and smiles at me with a glint of mischief in his eyes.

"Oh, for heaven's sake, sign the check!" says Judy.

Bob laughs. "If you hurry up, you can still take it off this year's income tax."

"Not that contribution," says Sam. "I don't think that group is very popular with the government."

"Is it midnight yet?" asks Barbara. "Someone tell me when it's midnight, I'm going to kiss all the men." She reaches across the sofa and squeezes Dennis's knee. He winces.

"There's nothing wrong," insists Jake, "with Sally explaining what she touches me for."

"Oh, stop it," says Judy. "We got all the literature in the mail just like everyone else. It's to stop the torture of political prisoners all over the world."

"But what does it *do*?"

"Right now," says Sam, "their function is informative, just trying to let people know what's going on, who's responsible, and the extent of it. Right, Sally?"

I nod.

"So," Jake says, imitating my nod, "you've shifted your emphasis to political prisoners." He smiles kindly...which, for Jake, means a bit condescendingly.

"Not at all," says Bob. "She already got nine or ten letters answering the Christmas cards she sent to ordinary...criminal prisoners, if you want to call them that. One answer was ten pages long, right, Dear?" He tightens his arm around my shoulders and looks at me proudly.

Jake signs the check and hands it to me. "But this time you'll restrict your help to writing letters." He's not being ironic. His face is a bit anxious for me.

"Well, you have to draw the line somewhere," murmers Barbara. I look at her and she flushes and grabs Sam's wrist, turning his watch toward her. "Isn't it midnight yet?"

"One of the nicest things about Sally," says Sam, "is her inability to draw lines."

It is like lying in one of those whirlpool baths, with the motor churning up waves of warm water all around my body. My friends making warm waves of love around me. Good people. Yes. Good people. And Bob, firmly encircling me with his arm. I don't look at him yet, not much, not directly into his face, but soon I will be able to. I've almost forgotten already. I shall forget.

"I just don't see," says Judy, "how you go on doing so much. Aren't you afraid she'll overdo it?"

"Hell, no," says Bob, giving me another squeeze. "The only time I worry about her is when she stops, the way she did the past month. But now she's in motion, almost her old self again, now that. . ." He lets the unfinished sentence hang there. Now that Gary's gone.

"It's been a rotten year," says Barbara.

"The election," says Jake.

"And your mother's death," Dennis murmurs gently. They all look at me, and I feel ridiculous, being pitied for the year's one bit of good luck: that Mother died quickly and painlessly before she became total pain to herself and to me.

Judy shakes her head. "Poor Sally, with all that, and the Gary business. . ." Now the name has been mentioned, and Gary becomes a huge presence in the room.

Bob laughs. "You know, Jake, John agrees with you. He told Sally she should stick to political prisoners. He said—get this, coming from him—he said, 'They're a better class of people'." Everyone laughs uncomfortably, knowing it's all right to laugh at John, but not sure whether they ought to laugh at that kind of joke.

"Is John out with his friends tonight?" asks Judy. "I kind of miss him. The last of our kids. Oh, except yours, Sam." Everyone glances at Sam, whose children we forget because he so seldom is allowed to see them.

"John's gone," says Bob. "Moved out."

"Really? Wasn't that rather sudden?"

Bob nods. "We said the magic words."

"What are they?"

" 'Get a job.' We gave him a month to find work and move out. Within two days he had a job and an apartment."

Silence again. This little detour has not exorcised the presence filling the room. Judy sighs. "I did sort of like Gary. I'm surprised you weren't able to reach him, Bob."

"Why me?"

"Well, you came from the same background. You know what it is to be poor. I thought. . ."

Bob shakes his head. "The minute I saw him, I recognized him. Look, among the poor, there are the kids who do paper routes and the kids who steal the money from them. I was the former, and Gary, the latter. And never the twain shall meet."

"But he wasn't that way anymore, not by the time he came here."

Bob nods. "That's true. He was in another place. I know that place too." He looks at me. "When Sally brought me home to meet her folks, I felt...like a worm compared to them. That made me really start to educate myself, read like crazy, ask questions, trying to bring myself up to them." He laughs. "Which I never quite managed to do, in their eyes, but that's another story." Now he frowns. "When Gary came here, I could see the struggle, because I'd been through it. Love and hate. Love, and the desire to emulate, to learn and grow more like the superior one. Hate, and the urge to destroy whoever shows up your inadequacy. I fell in love with Sally in the midst of fighting with her, hating her because she showed me how shallow and stupid I was. Luckily for me, love won over hate."

"While in Gary's case. . . ." Jake begins.

"Hate was stronger," finishes Bob.

Jake frowns. He doesn't like people finishing his thoughts for him. "All that proves is the depth of his feelings of inadequacy. I think it must have been deeper than anything you ever experienced."

"I'm surprised to hear you defend him," says Bob. "You washed your hands of him pretty fast."

"Oh, well." Jake leans back and smiles comfortably. "That was because I saw quite clearly what was happening. He behaved precisely the way self-hating people do, with complete consistency, testing the people who help them, testing, testing, until they alienate them. As if they have already judged themselves unworthy and, therefore, do things that will enlighten the innocent person who helps them. Very common. Gary's pattern was almost classic."

How well he talks. How well they all talk. Reasonable. Tolerant. Informed. It is a ritual. Taming experience with words. Analyzing defeat into insight. Where would we be without our words.

Bob is eager to agree. "I've seen it in some of my students. It is like a test. When I've taken an interest in one who's been in trouble, things go along all right for a while, and then they mess up. As if they're asking, will you still love me if I do this? and this? and this? Until I finally give up on them."

166

"And," finishes Jake, "free them from the demands made upon them by your expectations."

"Aren't you two forgetting something?" says Judy. Her voice trembles. "That kid spent over two years in prison!"

"Best thing that ever happened to him," Jake snaps. "If he hadn't been in prison, he wouldn't have attracted Sally's attention. He'd have just gone on squalidly but quietly throwing away his life."

"You're heartless!" Judy's eyes fill with tears. "He was locked up. Caged. And you expect him to come out and not show any effects of the hell he went through. There isn't anyone here who has any idea of what he went through! No one here has the right. . . ."

"Sam has," says Barbara. "Sam has the right."

Everyone turns toward Sam, but Sam puts his hands up as if pushing them gently away. He shakes his head and says, "I don't think you can compare. . . ."

"Of course not," says Judy, the tears overflowing. "Sam went in with more and came out with more."

Everyone waits for Sam to tell us his story again, to tell us what he went in with and came out with. But Sam surprises us.

"Maybe the great enemy is Freedom."

We're all stunned, as if Sam has uttered an obscenity. Of all the words we use so well, this one is most sacred.

"Didn't the old mystics say true freedom, perfect freedom, lies in obedience?" Everyone always looks uncomfortable when Sam starts quoting religious writers. Maybe that's why he doesn't usually talk much. "It was only when I gave up freedom that I found it. When I committed myself, completely and unquestioningly, to one principle. . . until then, life was. . .impossible."

"But your freedom lay in choosing what to submit to," says Jake, re-establishing balance, saving the sacred word.

If Mother were here, she would say, "There's right and there's wrong, and everyone chooses. That's your freedom. Right or wrong." And we would all ignore her.

Dennis makes an impatient move with both hands, as if he would sweep all the words away, and I see he is almost bursting. "Forget economics and class structure and all your psychological cliches! Nothing in your philosophy explains the demon that is driving him. It's a hard demon, ugly, a bit mad. It won't let him fit in anywhere, rest anywhere. It will keep him on the run. It will devour him. And when it does, he won't be Gary Wilson, delinquent or ex-con or anything else. He'll be a poet, an artist.

All silent, listening to the echo of Dennis's deep, dark voice. We'll stay silent out of a kind of embarrassment. No one wants to say that everywere Dennis looks he sees a poet, and every problem he sees is one of expression.

But Jake is in a fiendish mood tonight. "So one of these days he'll be a great poet—if he doesn't destroy himself first—and we'll all remember that we knew him during the early struggles with his demon. Maybe. Or maybe he's just an ordinary fuck-up who stumbled on a means to get attention, clinging desperately to an identity temporarily in fashion."

Bob, always eager to agree with Jake, laughs and nods. "The Prisoner Poet. Genius languishing in a cell. I bet the amount of paper being covered with bad poetry in prisons will wipe out the last of our forests."

Judy moans. "Oh, you two should be ashamed. No one has the right to ridicule anything a prisoner does to stay alive!"

Bob looks at me and flushes. I must be giving him a very severe look. "Of course, I'm sorry," he says. "That was a bad joke. I didn't mean it. I wish him well. I hope he makes me eat every bad word I ever said about him." He raises his glass. "I drink to Gary. May he prosper." He takes a sip, glances at me to see if he is forgiven. "Everyone's had his say about him, except you, Barbara."

Barbara shrugs. "I found him no different from most men."

Jake gives her his most wicked grin. "A real son of a bitch, eh?"

"Twelve o'clock!" shouts Judy. "Happy New Year!"

"Happy New Year, everybody!"

* * *

"OH." WHAT do I say to her? "You're down here."

She just looks at me. She holds the dog by the fur around his neck. Not a sound out of either of them, but that dog is pointed at me like a bullet.

"He'd still kill me if he could."

"Quiet, Yossarian, sit. Good dog. Sit."

"I just came for my things."

"Yes."

168

She's sitting on my bed, her back to the wall, a blanket pulled over her legs, reading something, some papers. Papers scattered all over the blanket. She watches me while I grab things and throw them into my suitcase and box. The room has been cleaned. All my stuff is piled on the table and chair.

"I thought I'd be in and out before anyone woke up."

"Did you?" She glances at her watch. It's almost five. You know I'm always awake before five."

"I forgot."

"Did you?" She looks at me for a while. "I thought maybe you wanted to see me."

"What for?"

"Maybe there was something you wanted to say to me."

"No."

She opens her mouth like she's going to say something else, but then closes it. Then she almost smiles. "If you'd come a couple of hours sooner you'd have walked into the middle of a party."

"Like the first time."

"Yes."

"Same people."

"Yes."

"All your good friends."

"Yes. They are. Good friends. Good people." Her voice is hard. Every word has a sharp edge. Then she sighs, and the sigh turns into a yawn. She is wearing her reading glasses. She pulls them off to rub her eyes. Deep, sagging pouches. She looks old.

"Did they talk about me?"

"Yes."

"What a rat I am? Ungrateful. Worthless."

She shakes her head. "They tried to explain."

"Oh, did they." It's not really a question, not a challenge. I don't want to argue. Neither does she. Not at five o'clock in the morning.

"Not to blame you . . . not to blame anyone."

"Just to explain me. Completely. Did they?"

She shakes her head. "Not completely. But . . . not too badly. Mainly to sooth me."

Yes, her friends are good at that. I can imagine it. Words. They have lots of words. For all occasions, like it says on the greeting-card rack.

"Have you found a place to stay?"

I nod. "Friends of mine in San Francisco. The ones I went to see at Thanksgiving."

"Do you think that will work out?"

"It's only temporary, till I get a place."

"How will you . . ." She stops and looks down at the papers in her hand, as if she has decided she shouldn't ask too many questions.

"I've got a couple of nights a week, hamburger place, washing dishes. Not much money, but all I want to eat."

"Hamburgers?" Her eyes widen.

"Something else will turn up." I close the lid of my suitcase. My books are in the box.

"It seems such a hard way."

I shrug.

"So unnecessary, when you could have skipped all that and . . ."

"Maybe it is necessary," I tell her. "Maybe you don't skip anything."

"You don't believe that."

"I don't know."

"But you are, anyway, more . . . comfortable . . . doing it this way?"

"I've never been comfortable in my life."

"No." She nods her head and just looks at me.

I put the front door key down on the table next to the typewriter. She nods.

"I ought to know where you are." I don't answer. "To forward mail. Or in case your parole officer calls."

"What will you tell him?"

"That you're not in. That'll be true. Then I'll give you the message and you can call him."

I'm glad she thought of it. I didn't. I nod and write the phone number and address on the top sheet of the stack of paper next to the typewriter. I bend to pick up my suitcase and box, but she is holding the papers out to me.

"Maybe you want to take these too."

"What? What's that?"

"Our letters." She's watching my face.

"No. I don't want them."

"What shall I do with them?"

"I don't care. Burn them."

"You don't even want to look at them? This one, for instance, that

170

you wrote only last March. Listen..."

"No, I don't want to hear."

"Why not?"

I shake my head.

"You're trembling," she says.

"It's cold." Why don't I just leave?

"After the party," she says, "I remembered where they were—still on the bookshelf, in the living room, where I put them the night you arrived. I brought them down here. I started from the beginning. I had almost finished when I heard you coming. Up the path, up the stairs. Down here, of course, you know who's coming before they ever reach the front door. No matter how quiet they try to be." She puts down the letter she is holding and looks at the bed, at all the letters scattered over her, burying her, covering her the way the old winos cover themselves with newspapers to keep warm. "Who do you think they are?"

I pretend I don't know what she means.

"I mean the two people who wrote these letters. Where did they go?"

I don't answer. I should just grab my things and go, but I don't, I can't.

"Are they all lies?"

"If you want to think that..."

"No, I don't want to." She shakes her head. "But I guess...they were only a part of the truth, that was the trouble."

"They were the whole truth while I was writing them."

She squints at me like she can't see me clearly. "I don't understand. You were..." She touches a sheet of paper with her finger. "...this man? Wholly?"

Well, what else could I be? With walls and bars and guards all over me. I haven't felt much like that man for a long time. Where is he? I feel like all the rest of me ran away and left him there in that cell. Oh, Jesus, if that's true—no, I won't think that. I won't think about that at all. I make myself yawn. I make my voice sound bored. "It's too early in the morning to start another analysis of what's wrong with me."

"I was just trying to understand," she says. Her voice is weak and she looks like a little girl under all those papers. She's not looking at me anymore, just at the letters scattered all over.

"Ask your friends, they like explaining things." As I pick up my things, she sits up straight and starts gathering up the letters.

"Well, if you don't want them, I'll keep them," she says. "And some day, reading them, one by one, I'll understand."

"One by one," I echo. It makes me think of her knitting. "Did you ever finish that cap you were knitting?"

"Yes. Not in time for Christmas, as I wanted to, but somehow I did finish it. Yes." She says it like the world would come to an end if she didn't finish whatever she started, even a woolen cap.

"I guess you'll know better what to start next time."

"What do you mean?"

"You know. Stick to knitting caps. They work out better."

"Better than people? You sound like Jake. He thought I shouldn't write to any prisoners this Christmas."

"But you did?" She nods. "What in hell for?" She doesn't answer me. "Christ, no matter what happens, you don't learn or change, you just keep doing the same thing over and over, even if you never get anywhere."

She takes a long time to answer, but when she does, she looks at me hard, the way I looked at that guard who told me I'd be back. "Sometimes if you can't get anywhere, the only way to keep from going backwards is to keep doing what you do, in spite of what you learn." Tough. God, she's tough.

"Yeah. I know what you mean."

"Do you?"

I don't know whether I do or not. Maybe I mean something different. I don't know. I only said it so she wouldn't have the last word. It doesn't matter. She's not looking at me for an answer. She's just picking up the letters and making a neat pile of them. "Well," I tell her, "it's your dungeon again."

"Yes."

I watch her for a minute, but she doesn't raise her head to look at me again.

Climbing up the stairs isn't bad, but once I'm outside it's cold and pitch black. I stumble on the rocky steps and the slick, muddy path, with some of the branches of trees whipping my face. My hands are full, so I can't push away the branches or catch myself when I trip. I hope I can get all the way down without falling.

Worst of all is the tiny light in the dungeon window. She is sitting there listening to my steps, maybe watching from the window.

Then the light goes out, and we're both in the dark.

172

EPILOGUE

Dear Sally,

My lawyer told me he would contact you right away about this farce, but I cant afford to take chances so I am following up with this letter. Even if he has given you the basic facts, I know you wont mind getting them again.

I was a passenger in a friends car when he was stopped for "speeding" (40 miles an hour! He's an outside co-ordinator for Prisoners United and gets stopped at least once a week). When they started to search the car, I told them that was illegal. They hit me, then showed me some pot on the back seat. I said I knew they planted it, and got roughed up some more for my trouble. We were booked and locked up, and they got a warrant to search our apartment.

At the apartment they found the tape recorder Barbara gave me. She had listed it with the things stolen last December, and it was registered with the Berkeley police. I tried to tell them it was a mistake that could be cleared up in five minutes, but no one wanted to listen.

They must have broken all records, getting an order revoking parole pending a hearing on charges of burglary (they want to charge me with six or seven others committed in your area at that time) resisting arrest, dope dealing, and, of course, violation of parole. They put me here, 150 miles from The City, where its hard for my lawyer to get to me.

I think I know why. Ive been trying to form a group of ex-con poets to publish a magazine of prisoners writing, some of it smuggled out of prisons. It probably doesnt add up to much and wont really change anything, but, as you always say, a person has to do something. Like knitting—enough stitches maybe add up to something in time. The trouble is it attracted attention to me, the kind of attention that spells trouble.

First of all we need a statement from Barbara saying she made a mistake when she put the tape recorder on the list. Thats the easy part. Maybe she has already done it.

My parole officer is willing to say that except for moving without telling him, I have been clean.

As to the dope charge, it may or may not be dismissed, depending on what judge I get and how he feels about radicals. If he is one of those who lump together demonstrators, organizers, not saluting the flag, dope, and dirty feet, I may not have a chance.

On the other hand, says my lawyer, all the prisons are so crowded and ready to blow up, that they dont want to put a man in if they can help it. Even the fact that I am known as an agitator could make them want to keep me out. They might be content with just hasseling me this far, might be almost ready to let me go.

In other words, situation normal, unpredictable, irrational and insane. Nothing has changed. It has only gotten worse. One thing is sure. If I am left for long in this place, I will never come out. I cant give details, but you can believe that I do not exaggerate if you remember some of the things I told you when I was out.

I am sure that after that Peoples Appeal lawyer was shot by an ex-con and especially after the latest prison riots, your friends warned you not to have anything to do with people like me. I also am sure that you will not listen to them because you know that I have never done anything violent and have never lied to you.

Help must come from outside. My lawyer says he knows you, or knows of you, and if I could get you busy on my case I would have a good chance. He says I need ''strong statements of support and interest, of your belief in my ability to function well outside, observed evidence of my full rehabilitation, continued interest in my development, etc.'' Maybe he already called you, and, if I know you, you have already started to do what is needed.

I wish now that I had taken your letters with me when I left to go out on my own. There have been many times these past few months when reading them over would have made my way easier. And now as I lay on my bunk trying to write (we are stacked three to a cell here, not even a place to stand) I wish I had them here to remind me that human decency still exists.

Please answer this letter as soon as possible so that I will know it has reached you.

Love,

Gary

P.S. Sally, I know you wont fail me. You are my only hope.

BOOKS BY DOROTHY BRYANT

ELLA PRICE'S JOURNAL

At thirty-five Ella Price enters college for the first time and begins an exciting and sometimes agonizing development. She not only records her changes but, by that very process, creates them.

MISS GIARDINO

Anna Giardino wakes up in a hospital unable to remember who injured her near the school where she had taught for forty years. Her returning memories explore complex issues and reveal the heroism in an "ordinary" life.

THE KIN OF ATA ARE WAITING FOR YOU

Ata is an island governed by the dreams of its people. Myth, scripture and psychology are woven into a mystical allegory which offers principles for spiritual growth and hope for a world where they might prevail.

THE GARDEN OF EROS

Starting with the first pain of her first childbirth, Lonnie, a young blind woman, lives through her ordeal alone, discovering her strengths while she relives and transcends the problems posed by the limitations of her life.

PRISONERS

Sally, 50, a Berkeley activist, and Gary, 25, a convict, begin a correspondence which knits them together in a struggle to free him. But can their relationship survive freedom?

WRITING A NOVEL (non-fiction)

From raw material, through planning, rough draft and revision, Bryant draws on her own experience and on that of many other writers to offer help to beginning writers of fiction.

BOOKS BY DOROTHY BRYANT

Non-fiction
WRITING A NOVEL (paper) $5.00

Novels
ELLA PRICE'S JOURNAL (cloth $10.00

THE KIN OF ATA ARE WAITING FOR YOU (paper) $5.00

MISS GIARDINO (paper) $6.00

THE GARDEN OF EROS (paper) $6.00

PRISONERS (paper) $6.00
            (cloth) $10.00

Order from

Ata Books
1928 Stuart Street, Berkeley, California 94703
Add $1.00 postage and handling for one book, 25¢ for each additional book.
Californians add 6% sales tax.